TALES FROM THE

Haunted Mansion

AUTUMN PUBLISHING

AUTUMN
PUBLISHING

Published in 2019
by Autumn Publishing
Cottage Farm
Sywell
NN6 0BJ
www.igloobooks.com

Autumn is an imprint of Bonnier Books UK

1219 001
2 4 6 8 10 9 7 5 3 1
ISBN 978-1-78905-629-7

Printed and manufactured in Italy

⚘ TALES FROM THE ⚘

Haunted Mansion

VOLUME III
GRIM GRINNING GHOSTS

Transcribed by **John Esposito**
as told by mansion librarian **Amicus Arcane**
Illustrations by **Kelley Jones**

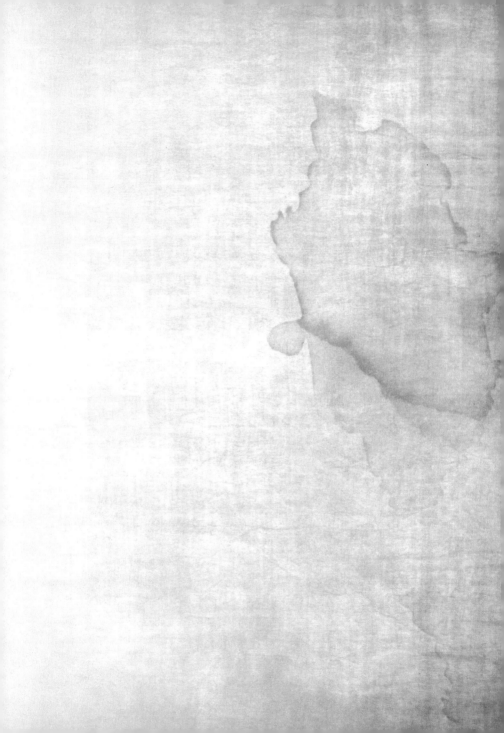

Third Time's the Harm

I'VE BEEN WAITING FOR YOU, FOOLISH READER.

❧

Call it a hunch. A premonition. A feeling in my guts. Oh yes,
something in my glowing grey matter told me you'd be back.
What is it they say? Third time's the charm.

Or is it 'Third time's the harm'?

No matter. What's of utmost importance is that you've
returned, momentarily safe and snug in your reader's space,
for more troubling tales of mystery, madness and the
macabre: three of life's — and death's — darkest delicacies.
And it is the number three with which we concern ourselves
today, for this is volume three, and three also happens to be
the most powerful number in the rarefied realms of magic and
the occult sciences.

It is no mere coincidence that a witch's spell is invoked in
repetitions of three. Shall we try one?

Very well. In a solemn voice, repeat after me:

I shall read this book, I shall read this book, I shall read
this book.

There now, it seems to be working.

What else comes in threes? Let's see. There are three wishes, three blind mice, three musketeers. Then there are the three parts of our day: morning, noon and night. The three phases of our lives: beginning, middle and end.

Ah, the end. Now we're getting somewhere. Those pitiable final moments. I refer, of course, to life's constant companion: death. A subject most near and dear to my non-beating heart.

Death comes in threes.

And fours and fives and so-ons. Death comes for everyone. Sometimes sooner rather than later.

Oh dear, there I go raising my hopes again. Not to worry, foolish reader. You're quite safe... for now. We here at the mansion need your kind — the kind with a pulse — to share our tales with the living.

So enter freely. Pass through our spiked gates, hear the cry of the raven and roam our cavernous corridors, where doors breathe and walls have eyes. Where the things that haunt your dreams are real...

And death is only the beginning.

Enter, foolish reader. I knew you'd come. There's no turning back now.

———— ✺ ————

Chapter One

X MARKS THE ROT

The mansion is an anomaly.

By all appearances, it was constructed with care, under the strictest of guidelines. It stands on a hill – whose name remains unspoken – where it has stood for over a century, protected by a wrought iron gate of uniform height. Only invited guests are permitted entry. And of those, only a privileged few are said to remain.

It is often labelled by its mysterious attributes. The mansion has been called enchanted and possessed. Some believe its unhallowed halls are host to refugees from the world of the living. Whatever its true nature, the mansion continues to intrigue and inspire.

The exterior is no more menacing than that of most homes of substantial girth. It is handsome to the naked eye, with boundless artistry and well-tended grounds. Maintenance crews, however, seem curiously scarce. Some see it as a Southern antebellum; others claim it was built in the style of a Dutch Gothic; still others see a Victorian manor on a hill. A nearby cemetery features grave markers from a bygone era – some with amusing epitaphs – and granite angels and finely sculpted cherubs of varying sizes.

The mansion is a favoured destination for writers of questionable taste and talents, a place to pen the great American ghost story. Or to live it. A harmless vocation by day.

But beware the night. For when the sun goes down, the true nature of the mansion is revealed, a nature that has secured its sinister reputation. Strange music occupies its hallways. Voices cry out from hidden chambers. The air is always chilled; the moon is always full. This is the mansion many call haunted.

Its precise history remains a mystery, concealed by fiction, contradicted by fact, one of a few glorious enigmas remaining in a world obsessed with origin stories.

CHAPTER ONE

There are some who claim it began as the residence of a certain Lord Gracey – heir to the Gracey fortune – who died under unusual circumstances. His body was discovered hanging under a skylight in the main foyer.

Others cling to the tale of a merciless sea captain, whose treasures remain hidden within the mansion's walls, along with the body of his late wife.

Still others suggest the mansion was designed by a mad genius for the sole purpose of transforming it into a deadly amusement park, for its secret passages and ingenious contraptions are without peer.

While its true origins remain elusive, some facts are beyond refute. For example, owing to its curious altitude, the mansion cannot be located by GPS. Nor has it been featured on conventional maps.

The famous parapsychologist Rand Brisbane spent ten years trying to pinpoint its exact location. The mansion he had erroneously labelled Gracey Manor had become his obsession, the holy grail of haunted investigations, until, finally, having wrangled an invitation by way of seance, Brisbane spent a single evening inside.

He was discovered the next morning wandering nearby Route 13, speaking gibberish. Brisbane was confined to a padded room in Shepperton Sanitarium, where he later died.

But before expiring, he had a map to the mansion tattooed on his leg from memory. Like many facets of the legendary mansion, the tattoo has since been dismissed as myth, an urban legend. However, one curious fact endures. The pathologist's official autopsy report for Rand Brisbane notes a patch of skin, approximately six inches by twelve inches, 'missing' from the upper portion of his left thigh.

Last week in the port of New Orleans Square, three shipping crates arrived by freighter. The ship's captain had been hired by proxy to secure land transportation to an undisclosed destination. He was provided with a map and paid handsomely to keep the details private. The captain had never seen a map like it.

It was composed of human flesh.

Chapter Two

THE RAVEN'S INN

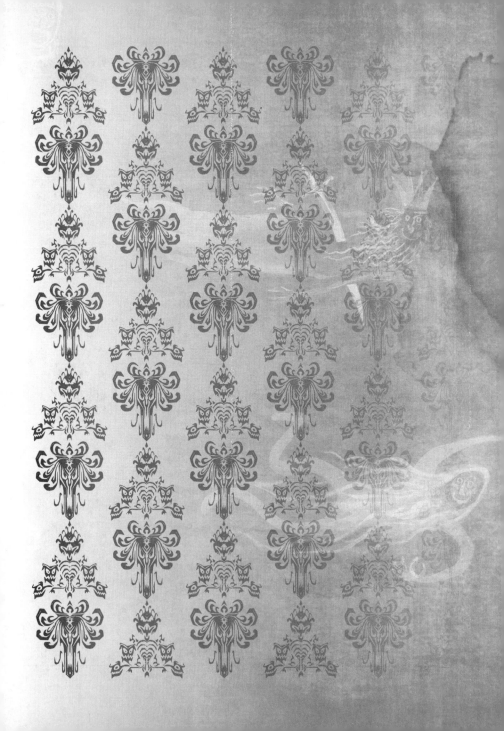

You wouldn't go there if you didn't have to. Not even if you'd been invited. *Especially if you'd been invited. You'd be begging for trouble if you did.*

The tall, brutish man with bulging biceps and one good eye shoved open the saloon-style doors, practically tearing them off the hinges. You might forgive Declan Smythe for not knowing his own strength, except that after five years of pumping iron in the prison courtyard, he actually knew it. If he hit the doors just right, they'd go flying. And with a little luck, the bouncer would get in his face and fists would fly, too. Declan Smythe loved a good fight, but not nearly as much as he loved a dirty one.

The Raven's Inn, located on Pier 33 in New Orleans Square, was known for that sort of clientele – the sort that threw punches before giving compliments.

Declan had been raised tough on the mean streets of Chicago. Before turning ten, he made his living as a street hustler. When he was eleven, he did his first stint in a young offender institute for beating up the school head teacher. That was bad enough, but Declan Smythe didn't even go to school. He just beat up a head teacher.

Big-boy prison had done very little to reform his wild ways. On the third Friday after his release, he returned to the scene of so many past indiscretions, the Raven's Inn. There was that familiar crunch of broken teeth and sawdust under his boots, the smell of burnt chicken wings in the air. Declan Smythe was home. He went straight to his usual seat at the bar; at least, it had been his usual seat five years earlier. The man on the stool glanced over his shoulder. "What can I do ya for, big fella?"

"You're in my seat."

"So? Go find another one."

"You first."

CHAPTER TWO

Before the man knew it, he was sailing through the saloon doors, which, much to Declan's delight, did indeed fly off the hinges. No one said a word, not even the bouncer. It must have been the extra thirty pounds of muscle Declan had put on since he'd been away.

He reclaimed his stool and pounded the counter. A flat-nosed bartender came over straight away, remembering Declan from the old days. As if he could forget. Declan was the one who'd flattened his nose. The bartender put on his best *glad to see ya* face. "Declan Smythe, when did they let you out?"

"Three weeks ago, chief."

"You'll want your usual." The bartender lifted a cheap libation from under the counter.

Declan shook his head. "Been off the sauce for years. What I'm really dreamin' about is a cup of Tusk's Tasty Tanis Tea."

"Keep dreamin'," said the bartender. "They don't make that brand no more."

"No way!"

"Yes way. A lot's changed since you been away, Deck."

Declan gave the tavern the once-over. There were faces he did not recognise, music he had never heard. Yes, the world had moved on without him, taking his job and his home along with it. If things didn't turn around soon, the toughest tough guy in New Orleans Square might be living in a cardboard box. But his luck was about to change. Notice we didn't say 'for the better'.

Oh, I noticed.

He saw her sitting across the bar. She looked exactly the same as he remembered, and – forgive us for saying – 'the same' wasn't a good thing.

Says who? Beauty is in the eye of the beholder.

Marge Mulvaney had the kind of face that looked randomly pieced together by a particularly cruel child. And if you switched the parts round, it would come out even worse. Her eyes were mismatched, and her nose dribbled over her cleft lip like candle wax.

Declan headed her way as patrons backed up to keep from being trampled. Once in range, he gave Marge a friendly swat on the back. She spit out the sandwich she'd just put in her mouth, chopped meat and caramelised onions splattering all over the counter. "Whoever you are, get ready to spit teeth!" She cocked her fist and turned. Her face lit up when she saw him. (It didn't help.) "Declan Smythe! I thought they put you away for good!"

"Nope. They put me away for bad!" They exchanged

CHAPTER TWO

old-pal hugs, during which Declan inadvertently adjusted her bad back. "Early release. Would ya believe on 'good behaviour'?"

"No, I would not believe it!"

They laughed like they were back in the old days. "So what brings you back to this dive? I thought you got banned for life," he said.

Marge hesitated. She was there for a specific reason and was leery of sharing her good news. "Just wettin' my whistle. Anyhoo, it was great seein' ya again, Deck. Let's get together real soon, okay?"

Declan planted himself on the stool next to her, not going anywhere. "We're together now. What's goin' down, Marge? Tell me. Spill it. All of it."

"It's an honest job, Deck. I'm totally straight these days."

"Aces, Marge. Me too. Straight as a boomerang. Who's involved?"

She didn't want to say. Oh, how she didn't. But Declan wasn't the type to take no for an answer. "You remember Pasquale? The mover?"

Declan chuckled. "Skinny little nothin'. You still sweet on him?"

"I ain't sweet on nothin'! He owns a removals van. This old codger hired us to move some goods."

Declan stopped chuckling, at once interested. "What goods?"

"We don't know."

"What do you mean ya don't know?"

"It's all very mysterious, I tell ya."

Declan rested his oversized hand on Marge's shoulder; even without trying, he felt like he was pressing her into the ground. "Good news, Marge. You got yourself a partner."

"I already got a partner."

"Then this must be your lucky day, because now you got two. We'll be the three Mouseketeers."

"Musketeers."

"Whatever."

Marge saw the look in Declan's good eye. Refusing him was not an option. Besides, it might not be a bad idea. New Orleans Square was a rough spot, and Pasquale was about as menacing as Donald Duck. Marge stuck out her hand to shake. "Welcome aboard, partner. I'll pay you out of my share."

"That's awful generous of you, Marge. Just awful." They shook on it. "This delivery? Where's the drop off?"

CHAPTER TWO

Marge removed a wrinkled map (the one made from you-know-what) from her bag. "The place is in the middle of nowhere. Off Route 13." She slid the map across the counter for Declan to take a look. He touched its fleshy corner and shuddered.

"What in the world?"

"Pretty creepy, right? You never felt anything like it." But he had. Declan Smythe knew exactly what the map was made from. He'd been around dead bodies before.

Marge pointed to their final destination: a large dwelling situated on a hill. Declan nodded in approval. His good eye knew a good deal when it saw one. "A mansion," he whispered. "Jackpot!" Declan's good eye narrowed. "When?"

"Tonight. The old codger said the delivery had to happen between midnight and six."

Declan smiled. "Looks like we're workin' the graveyard shift."

It was past midnight, and Pier 33 was mired in a stew-like fog. Declan, Marge and Pasquale watched as a trio of dockers wheeled three large crates into the cargo hold of an old removals van. The crates ranged in size: the largest one was a piano case, with the return address Buena Vista Middle

School. The second one was an enormous oblong box with custom stamps from Valley of the Kings, Egypt. The third one was long and thin, a little bigger than your average front door. That label read *Salem, Mass.*

Pasquale had just been shown the map, and he was visibly shaken. "I just wanna go on record as sayin' this is a baaaaad idea. I knew a dude who knew a dude who went up there once. A long time ago."

"And?"

"And the dude went straight-up bonkers! They still got him locked up at Shepperton, along with the rest of the loonies. Laughing his brains out. Loonies love to laugh."

"That's malarkey!" declared Declan.

"He didn't know nothin' about malarkey. He only knew English." Pasquale gave the map another glance. "That's it, all right. It looks real fancy on the outside. Like a place you might dream about livin'. Except it ain't no dream, it's a nightmare. Because once you get inside, things change real fast. There are rooms with no doors and steps leadin' to nowhere. And it's always cold! Even when it's boilin' hot outside – so hot your feet can't even touch the sidewalk – this place is freezin'."

CHAPTER TWO

That didn't faze Declan. "Sounds like cross ventilation to me."

"I'm tellin' ya, he seen things," continued Pasquale. "And some of them things weren't very nice."

"*I'm* not very nice. Tell me, did he see any gold or jewellery up there?"

"I wouldn't know. But he mentioned the artwork. He said they got paintings that change when you stare at 'em."

"Then don't stare at 'em. It ain't polite to stare," Marge said as she managed a smile. "He's nuts, you said so yourself."

"Maybe." Pasquale nodded. "But the mansion didn't make him that way."

Now Marge's curiosity was piqued. "What in the world does that mean?"

"It happened later on, after he got home. They found him curled up behind his sofa. The dude was pointin' and laughin'. Just pointin' and laughin'. Loonies love to laugh."

"At what? Spill it! What was he pointin' at?"

"A mirror."

"A mirror?"

"That's right, a mirror."

"Any idea what he saw in there?" Declan asked. Then he added, "Besides his big dumb mug?"

"The dude's the only one who knows, and he ain't sayin'. He's just laughin'. But whatever he saw, it turned his mop full of black hair… pure white. In an instant. As white as fresh snow!"

The image made Declan chuckle. It was a nervous chuckle. Pasquale continued. "He did say somethin' strange while they was loadin' him into the loony van." Marge and Declan leant in to hear. Pasquale looked back at the mysterious crates entering his van. "He said a ghost had followed him home."

Chapter Three

THE PHANTOM MANOR

Pasquale's van chugged along the single-lane road, bucking like it had a bad case of hiccups. The van's headlights hadn't done much to penetrate the fog, and the reflection of the high beams only made it worse.

Pasquale was in the driver's seat. It was his van, after all. He had once earned an honest living as a removals man. Honest Man Movers was the company name; it still said so on the side of his van. But Pasquale had fallen on hard times and, to make ends meet, had resorted to making deliveries for questionable clientele, the kind one often came across in New Orleans Square.

"Is this piece of junk even gonna make it?" muttered Declan from the window seat. Poor Marge was crammed in the middle.

Pasquale squinted to see through the soupy fog. Gnarled branches from blackened trees were reaching down on both sides of the road. "She'll make it," he replied. But really, Pasquale wasn't so sure.

The conditions were, in a word, treacherous. And in two words, insanely treacherous. Apart from the lack of street lights, the road seemed to curve and twist and wind for the sake of curving and twisting and winding. There were no safety barriers. No reflectors. And situated every few yards were potholes the size of graves. Pasquale couldn't avoid them all, and the van swerved, sending the crates sliding and colliding.

"Careful," shouted Marge. "The old codger said the stuff needs to get there in one piece or we don't get paid."

But Pasquale was way ahead of her. "What's the good of gettin' paid if you ain't alive to spend it? They say Route 13 is haunted."

CHAPTER THREE

Declan groaned. "Oh no, not another 'dude who knew a dude' story!"

"No. This one's first-hand. A lot of people croaked on this road, which is why it don't appear on no map. Route 13 had an unusually high incident rate. It's been called the Bermuda Triangle of highways."

"What's this got to do with anything Bermuda?" Marge asked.

"The Bermuda Triangle is a place, a real one, where boats and airplanes have disappeared. For years and years. They went missing without a trace."

That put the whammy on Marge. "Okay, so I'm officially spooked. Turn this bad boy around. I ain't lookin' to disappear."

"I'm with ya," agreed Pasquale, nodding. His right foot must have also agreed, because it eased up on the accelerator, bringing the van to a crawl. "You see that?"

"See what?" Declan's full supply of patience, which was very small on a good day, had run out.

"Bats! Vampire bats are watching us from the trees!"

"There ain't no bats in these parts, no sir, nohow!"

Marge wiped condensation from the windscreen. "You might want to tell that to the bats." A family of oversized bats were hanging upside down from the gnarled tree branches and staring with ruby-red eyes.

"Okay," Declan conceded. "So there are bats. And fog and thunder and creepy trees. So what? There's also a pot o' gold waitin' at the end of this rainbow."

"What're you talkin' about?"

"Who lives in mansions? Rich folks, right? Rich folks live in mansions!" **They also die there.**

"Yeah, so?"

"So this job could be our one-way ticket out of the poorhouse. These places are loaded with jewellery and safes stuffed with cash!"

Pasquale nodded. "Yeah, they're loaded, all right. Mansions are loaded with security. These fat cats have fancy alarms and mean old guard dogs."

"And if we was breakin' and enterin', that would be a problem," said Declan. "But we ain't breakin' and enterin'. We're marchin' right through their fancy front door like we was invited, 'cause we was." **Getting in is easy. But getting out, Master Declan? That's a much graver proposition.**

Marge was no longer feeling lucky. She squeezed Pasquale's arm. "You were right. This is a bad road. Let's wait till it's light."

CHAPTER THREE

Wham! Declan's oversized fist slammed the dashboard. "We ain't waitin' for nothin'. The old goat said the delivery's gotta be at night, so we deliver at night." He pointed out something on the side of the road. "Besides, how bad can it be? Them three seem to be doin' just fine." Marge and Pasquale looked to see what he was pointing at.

There were three scruffy men – one tall, one husky and one diminutive with a beard – hitch-hiking, their thumbs extended.

"Should we pick 'em up?" asked Pasquale. He was such a softy.

"Not on your life!" **Or yours. Heh-heh.** "We ain't got time for good deeds."

Marge found herself agreeing with Declan, but not for the same reason. There was something off about the hitch-hikers, something not quite right. Maybe it had to do with the lighting? But there wasn't any! So how were they *glowing*?

Pasquale hit the accelerator and the van sped off. Checking his side mirror, he could see the road shrinking behind them. But the hitch-hikers, they were gone. *Poof!* Like *Bermuda Triangle* gone.

The van crept up to the mansion gates. It was just before two in the morning. The entrance was locked, with no one there to greet them. Pasquale was secretly relieved. "Well, that's that!" The mansion's location was a mystery no longer, but the gate was locked, and that was good enough for Pasquale. He checked his mirror, ready to back out.

Declan reached over and pinched Pasquale's shoulder. Hard. "Owwwww! That's gonna turn black and blue!"

"You're welcome," replied Declan as he shoved his head out the window. "Yo! Special delivery! Open up!"

They waited a few minutes. Nothing until… *reeeeeeeeeeee!* The front gates opened with a grind that gave them goose pimples. Marge elbowed Pasquale, right on his brand-new black and blue. "I don't like this."

"Ow. I'm with ya."

Declan had heard just about enough out of both of them. "Yo! Scaredy-cats! They're invitin' us in, just like I said."

Marge asked, "Who's 'they'?"

He pointed. "Them's 'they'."

A scraggly looking man clutching an old-fashioned

lantern was making his way through the gate. There was a shivering bloodhound at his side. The van inched forwards, bringing them into speaking range. "Turn round," the man warned. "Visiting hours end at sundown."

"Says who?" blurted out Declan.

"Says me. I'm the caretaker around these parts. For more years than I wish to remember."

"Caretaker, eh? Well then, would ya mind takin' care of them gates? We ain't visitin'. We're deliverin'!"

"By whose authority?"

Marge had the paperwork in her bag. She located the manifest and read a name from the bottom. "Arcane."

The caretaker reacted – boy, did he ever. So did the dog. Like someone had just pumped ice water through their veins. I'm flattered! "V-very well," the caretaker said with a shiver. "Follow the path to the back of the estate. You'll pass a graveyard on the right. The left, too. Do not stop. No matter what you see or hear, just keep moving."

Pasquale thanked him and drove on. But the caretaker never said *you're welcome*. As the van passed through the imposing gates, all he could manage was a remorseful "I'm sorry".

The van climbed the hilly path, spotlighted by a large harvest moon. As promised by the caretaker – and the map made from you-know-what – the Eternal Grace Cemetery took up a good portion of the hillside. Even through closed windows, the threesome could hear music coming from within the boneyard. It was a barbershop quintet. Declan bobbed his head, digging their tune. "Sounds like a parrrr-teeee!"

Pasquale turned to Marge. "Who throws a party in a graveyard?" **You'd be surprised. The dead do enjoy a good shindig.**

The music rising from the cemetery was much more than a mischievous melody. The lyrics were a foreshadowing of the woeful wonders yet to come. The quintet sang their hearts out. **And their lungs and their kidneys. You're invited to join them, of course. We're always on the lookout for one more... voice.**

"When the crypt doors creak
and the tombstones quake,
spooks come out for a swinging wake.
Happy haunts materialise
and begin to vocalise.
Grim grinning ghosts come out to socialise."

CHAPTER THREE

That was all Pasquale needed to hear. He hit the accelerator and sped away from the terrifying tune as quickly as he could.

A split in the road directly ahead prompted Pasquale to pull over to the side and check the map. "We're here and —"

Ss-kink! Ss-kink! Ss-kink! They all heard it. *Ss-kink! Ss-kink! Ss-kink!* Declan lowered his window, aiming a torch into the cemetery. "Now what was that?" Pasquale asked.

"None of our business, *that's* what!" responded Declan.

Oh, but he was wrong. **Dead wrong.** The beam of Declan's torch discovered the source of the *ss-kink*. There were three men **(no, not the hitch-hikers)** in matching tuxedos, standing knee-deep in dirt. *Ss-kink! Ss-kink! Ss-kink!* They had shovels. *Ss-kink! Ss-kink! Ss-kink!* They were digging! *Ss-kink! Ss-kink! Ss-kink!* Three separate graves!

"Gravediggers." Declan did his best to play it down. "Just doin' their jobs is all."

Pasquale pressed lightly on the accelerator, his van *chug-chug-chug*ing out of range. They were each thinking the same thing, yet only Marge had the gumption to question it out loud. "Who digs graves in the middle of the night?"

"They do," declared Declan. "Let's not make a ting out of it, okay?"

Pasquale swallowed – hard. "It's not their timin' that bugs me. It's the number of holes." He looked at his partners. "Why did it have to be *three* graves?"

The others remained silent. For once, even Declan Smythe was too creeped out to comment.

The van had backed into the first stall of the loading bay. A massive steel shutter slowly lifted to unveil the black-as-black entrance. It sounded like an enormous chain working a giant pulley. Declan, Marge and Pasquale wheeled the mysterious crates through the entrance on handcarts. Once they were inside, the shutter closed behind them with a rumble, its hollow *THWONG!* adding an unwanted finality to the moment. There was no turning back now – for them or you, foolish reader.

"What do we do now?" asked Pasquale, hoping one of the others had a clue, because his brain was on empty.

Declan took a cautious step forwards, illuminating the path with his torch. They had entered what resembled an immense warehouse attached to the back of the mansion, its dimensions undefinable, its contents indescribable. He couldn't find a single wall or even locate its ceiling. The space seemed to go on indefinitely. There were rows upon rows of shelves, some as tall as trees, and the shelves were loaded with crates, similar to the ones they'd brought, stamped with the names of exotic locations. Of particular interest to the morbidly curious – **and that would be you** – was the fact that the majority of the crates were rattling, as if the things inside were trying to become the things outside.

Even though they didn't know what this place was or what it meant, the threesome were genuinely gobsmacked. Mind you, they didn't even know what *gobsmacked* meant. But the sounds were enough. Between the incessant scratching and the moans and screams, there was little doubt. The sounds were inhuman.

"What in the world is this place?" asked Marge.

A voice emerged from the shadows: "I call it home." The tone of the voice wasn't sinister. In fact, one might call it welcoming. Like a spider welcoming a fly into its web. The threesome turned in circles, trying to locate its owner.

"It came from over there!"

"No, it's over there!"

"No, I'm over here." A gaunt figure was suddenly beside them, having materialised from a space between the shadows. "Allow me to introduce myself. I am the librarian." Declan aimed his light straight into the stranger's face, and Marge gasped. And just a reminder: Marge was a little bit on the gasp-y side herself. The figure standing before them was tall and thin, attired all in black, with a lit candelabrum in his gloved hand and a face more skull than skin.

"Good for you!" replied Declan. "But books ain't our ting."

"We were hired to drop off some merchandise," added Marge, having located her voice from somewhere in the pit of her stomach. "From Pier 33."

"Ah, yes." The librarian nodded his approval. "You have been expected, Mistress Marjorie." He shifted his candelabrum, bringing light to the three crates. "Welcome home."

"What is that supposed to mean?" asked Declan.

"All will be explained… at the proper time." He pointed to the crate by Pasquale, the one marked *Buena Vista Middle School*. "If you'd care to follow… this one resides in our music room."

Pasquale looked to the others. Gobsmacked. And that's how you learn a new word, kiddies.

Declan stepped between them. "Just a second, lie-berry man! The old codger at the pier said payment on delivery."

"Correct, Master Declan." The librarian raised his lantern, indicating a path between the shelves. "Once the items have been returned to their... proper resting places." He beckoned the threesome to follow.

Pasquale stepped protectively in front of Marge. "What's this all about? You say you're a librarian, but I don't see no books."

"Look around. Feast your eyes." The librarian made a sweeping gesture, indicating the crates. "There are stories everywhere you turn." The librarian then lowered the lantern and turned to face the three of them. "My name was" – he corrected himself – "*is...* Amicus Arcane. I am the mansion's keeper of tales."

"You also better be the keeper of the mansion's chequebook," snapped Declan, "or we got ourselves a problem." He flexed his biceps. You could hear his muscles rippling under his sleeves. "A big problem."

The librarian smiled, somewhat slyly. "Payment comes in other forms." He looked at the others. "This way to the music room. Oh, and mind your step. We wouldn't want anyone to depart… prematurely." He spun like a top and led the threesome into the uncharted darkness.

The music room was a shadowy chamber, save for a shaft of moonlight spying from a small skylight. It featured a treasure trove of musical instruments collected from around the globe. Also on display: a collection of tarnished music boxes, bastioned by a cover of spiderweb, and sheet music culled from the finest composers this world – and the next – has ever known. Phosphorescent dust particles danced about the air amid antique furnishings and somehow moved in time with a funeral dirge played on an organ, its whereabouts unknown.

The threesome wheeled the first crate through the entrance. "Where does it go?" asked Pasquale.

Declan pointed to a boldly coloured rectangle on an otherwise dull area rug, the obvious space for so large a piece. "Right there, genius."

"Precisely," replied the librarian. The threesome spun round to face him. Amicus Arcane, as he was known in life, was somehow suddenly standing behind them. He stepped forward, almost appearing to glide across the room rather than walk, and approached the threesome. "If you wouldn't mind?" He offered Declan a rusty crowbar.

"Mind? No, sir. I been achin' to find out what you got hidin' in here." The brute got busy removing the lid from the crate. The item was concealed under a forest of wood shavings. Marge dug through the top layer. Her entire face lit up when she saw what was under it, and Pasquale thought, *She's kind of pretty when she smiles.* With special emphasis on *kind of.*

"It's a piano!"

"So much for a treasure," groaned Declan, his hopes for a big pay day momentarily dashed.

"Do you play?" Pasquale asked Marge softly.

"I used to," Marge replied, almost shyly. "My parents made me take lessons when I was a little girl."

"Hard to believe," interjected Declan.

"That I was little?"

"That you was a girl!"

Pasquale shot her a smile. "I'd like to hear you sometime." And Marge thought, *He's kind of—*

"Awkwaaaard!" interrupted Declan, sticking his giant

melon-shaped head between them. "Looks like a hunk o' junk. Is it worth anyting?"

The librarian unleashed a ghoulish grin before covering his mouth with his hand, like he was hiding something. "Hard to say. How much are souls going for these days?"

"What's *that* mean?"

"Only that music soothes the soul," replied Amicus Arcane. "Perhaps you'll allow me to elaborate while you unpack." The librarian lowered himself into an antique chair like he was lowering himself into the grave, and he reached for a hardback book that had been waiting for him on a music stand. The book was covered in dust and bore no markings, save for a simple *Volume III* engraved on its spine.

As the threesome removed the handsome old piano from its crate, the librarian blew dust from the cover, then opened the book and began to read...

Interlude

Heed my warning, foolish mortal:

Proceed with caution.
They already know you're here.
They've had their eyes on you.
The ones with eyes, of course.
Our wall-to-wall creeps are always watching,
waiting for the right moment to reach out.
Just ask Mrs Birch.
That is, if you can find her.
Who is Mrs Birch, you might enquire?

Read on.

Before she finds you.

———— ❦ ————

Chapter Four

STRANGE MUSICALITY

Tobe was a naturally gifted musician. One might say he had an ear for music. Two of them, in fact. He had performed a piano sonata at the Buena Vista Middle School music semi-finals that would knock your ears off. If you'd been invited, of course. But you weren't. So you'll have to trust us on that. It was sublime.

The audience – students, teachers and parents alike – rose to their feet even before the final notes were played. The applause was thunderous, a six-minute standing ovation, the kind usually reserved for an established master in a place like Carnegie Hall. And to think that was only the warm-up…

The real event was scheduled for the following Friday: the Buena Vista Middle School music finals. A local TV station was planning to attend, even though the expected outcome was inevitable. The scholarship belonged to Tobe.

Afterwards, a line of admirers extended out the hall doors, a thirty-minute wait just to shake hands with the young maestro.

Tobe's third-grade piano teacher had been the first to recognise his gifts. Now that he was in his early teens, it wouldn't be a stretch to label him a wunderkind. A modern-day Beethoven, even. Sure, lots of kids his age can play an instrument, and play it well. But performing is a common talent. Composing, on the other hand – writing music as sophisticated as his semi-final sonata – put Tobe in a class all of his own.

Or did it?

A mousy freshman named Genevieve wasn't so sure, and she felt it was her moral obligation to set the record straight. So she stood in line, like everybody else, waiting for her chance to approach the young maestro. Now, in the interest of full disclosure, we should mention that Genevieve was also competing for the music scholarship. Although a gifted pianist in her own right, Genevieve had to concede she was not in the same musical league as Tobe. His talent was to be admired, and she had no interest in soiling his reputation. Still, she owed it to a friend to tell him what she knew. The sonata he'd taken credit for had actually been composed by someone else – someone who could no longer defend herself. **We'll see about that.**

The sonata had been composed by a corpse.

Not at the time, of course. Mrs Birch, the former music teacher at Buena Vista Middle School, had been very much alive when she wrote it. Genevieve had been there during its inception. Still, she would give Tobe the benefit of the doubt. Maybe he'd heard Mrs Birch randomly playing it down in the school archives and when it came time to compose his own piece, bits of the sonata seeped in from his subconscious. That would be one explanation. It happens all the time in art. The problem was his piece wasn't a little like Mrs Birch's. It was the *exact* same sonata, note for note, measure for measure. And Tobe had taken full credit for it, accepting all the accolades.

Just like he was about to accept the full scholarship.

So Genevieve waited her turn, a full thirty minutes in line, just to tell him: "That wasn't your music."

He peered down from the stage. His hair was wildly

unkempt, and he wore thick-rimmed glasses he didn't actually need. It was all part of a prefabricated look – the mad musical genius. He snapped his fingers, trying to come up with her name. "You are…?"

"Genevieve," said Genevieve. "I sit behind you in chorus."

"Not possible. I would have noticed those freckles."

Genevieve blushed. "It's possible. I'm not very noticeable."

But she was that night. She had delivered the first blow innocently enough, but not out of meanness. There wasn't a mean bone in her body. Scalpel, please. We'll check. Still, Tobe had to figure out a way to stop her, to shut Genevieve down before she said another word. The people lining up behind her – Tobe's fans – were already starting to gossip.

"Oh, wait!" He snapped his fingers again. "Now I remember. Didn't I help you out once? The winter concert. You were really killing it on the triangle."

She blushed a deeper shade, flattered that he remembered. "Yes, you were so very generous with your time."

The longest two minutes of my life, thought Tobe. "You're welcome." He gently took her hand to shake. "If you ever need any more help, you know who to ask." He tried to see past her, to the face of his next admirer, now on the approach. But Genevieve stayed where she was, and Tobe's false smile evaporated. The mad musical genius simply looked mad... as in *angry* mad. "I have a lot of fans to get through. Let's pick this up in chorus on Monday. Okey-doke?"

Genevieve nodded, turning to leave. But she couldn't. For Mrs Birch, she couldn't let it pass. Tobe's eyes narrowed under the fake glasses. "Still here?"

"The piece you played..." Genevieve swallowed whatever trepidation she had. "And, oh, you played it so well. Mrs Birch would have been honoured."

Tobe could no longer mask his feelings, his anger overflowing. He whipped off the glasses. "Mrs Birch? What are you talking about?"

Genevieve started blinking, which happened when she got upset. She needed to regroup. Stay strong. Stop blinking! If the fight had been hers, she would have already taken the dive. But she was fighting for a friend, one, as we noted, who could no longer defend herself. Genevieve took three deep breaths, like Mrs Birch had said to do when she got nervous. "Your piece..." she began. "It's really *her* piece. Maybe you didn't realise it. It was probably an innocent mistake. But I was there when she composed it. I volunteer in the archives. And that piece you said you wrote – it was actually written by her."

An admirer behind Genevieve gasped, and Tobe knew at once what he needed to do. He had to incite them, to set his fans on the mousy girl making all those not-so-ridiculous allegations. He knew the mousy ones weren't very good fighters. They didn't have it in them. That was why they didn't have fans. Oh, I might know one or two 'mouses' who do. All Tobe needed was the perfect mousetrap… along with the appropriate wedge of cheese. All right, enough with the mouse metaphor. It was time for Tobe to break out the bully tactics.

At once, he brought his voice down to a somewhat timid tone, matching it with an almost pitiable little-boy-lost look. His admirers had to lean in to listen. "You accused me of stealing. Of being a thief, a dirty cheat."

Before Genevieve could reply, an overwhelming murmur swelled from the crowd. *His* crowd. Here's the thing: the Buena Vista football team was zero and thirteen. Academically, the school was at the very bottom of an almost bottomless barrel. Tobe, their one ray of sunshine, was the only thing keeping it on any sort of map – flesh or otherwise. Attacking him was like attacking the school mascot. (Which happened to be a mouse. Go figure.) Even Principal Gribbons seemed out for blood as he swiftly approached the stage. "Is everything all right, Tobe? You look upset."

CHAPTER FOUR

"Is everything all right? I've just been accused of being a dirty cheat. Maybe I should drop out of the finals." He looked pleadingly to the crowd. "What do you say?"

"Nooooooo!" they replied in perfect harmony. Without Tobe, there would be no TV cameras. No headlines, except for the humiliating football scores. No anything. Their angry eyes turned to his accuser, Genevieve. She put up her hands in mouse fashion and attempted to explain. "You don't understand. No one admires Tobe more than I do. I never said he was a cheat."

"Yes you did!" someone cried out from the crowd. "I heard it too!" shouted someone else. And then came the ensemble: "So did I!" "Me too!"

Followed by the personal attacks from the balcony: "She's jealous! She'd do anything to win that scholarship!"

Followed by the chants: "Throw her out! Throw her out! Throw her out!" The sound was deafening. Genevieve couldn't plead her case over the roar of the angry crowd. She looked to Principal Gribbons for support. He had implemented the district's Zero Tolerance for Bullies policy, after all. How dispiriting, then, to see him leading the chant, conducting with his hands: "Throw her out! Throw her out! Throw her out!"

Genevieve ran from the stage, fearing for her life. Angry mobs can threaten that. **Especially in horror stories.** Tobe took centre stage and, in a soothing voice, explained that it wasn't Genevieve's fault. She was merely using every means necessary to win the scholarship, even if it meant smearing the competition. This elicited even more support, the crowd affording Tobe a seven-minute ovation – shattering the old record! In the eyes of his admirers, Tobe was a true champion of the people.

He had silenced the competition, and no one would stand in his way. The only other soul to know the truth was dead. And the dead aren't very noisy. Corpses by and large keep to themselves, snug in their graves. Every now and then, however, you come across a noisy one. The kind that rattle chains in your attic or go creaking about in cupboards. If you're lucky, the noises stop on their own. If you're not so lucky, the noises do what they did to Tobe.

The young maestro was about to hear from a noisy spirit, indeed. A spirit with a score to settle.

Mrs Birch died in the music archives, where she had spent most of her days. The cause of death had not been shared with the student body, but that didn't stop anyone from

CHAPTER FOUR

guessing. Several theories slithered their way into canteen chit-chat. For example: Mrs B had died with her eyes wide open, which is fairly common, along with her mouth, as if she was in the middle of a song, which is less common.

Or had she died screaming?

Her fingers had still been touching the piano keys. Tinkling the ivories, as it were. Putting these two things together, it would appear she had died doing what she loved. Singing at the piano. *Phew!* **Sounds like a pleasant way to go, doing what you love, unless you love bullfighting; that would be painful... and messy.**

Oh, and there was one other thing – a minor detail, but one you should hear. The police had kept it out of the news, but Mike Shea, whose mum worked as a dispatcher, had got the info straight from the corpse's mouth. **(Not literally.)** It appeared Mrs Birch had been discovered on her piano stool with her head turned completely round, facing backwards.

At this point it's only fair to interject: canteen chit-chat is traditionally prone to exaggeration. Gross exaggeration. But as it applies to canteen cuisine, chit-chat can also provide a reasonable distraction from the cardboard squares being pawned off as pizza. The reality was no one really knew how Mrs Birch had died. Well, except for Mrs Birch and, of course, the caretaker, who had discovered her remains, and he wasn't talking. Canteen chit-chat said that he went insane, that he currently mopped the floors of the crazy house… out of habit.

One thing was certain, confirmed during a double-period assembly in the main hall: Mrs Birch had died in the archives, and the door had been sealed with an industrial-strength lock and a heavy chain.

Unusual security measures, wouldn't you say? Were they worried about someone getting in? Or *something* getting out?

Genevieve would be the first to tell you there was absolutely nothing to be afraid of. **And I have 998 spirited acquaintances who'd insist she was wrong. Dead wrong.** She knew Mrs Birch about as well as she knew herself. They'd spent an exceptional amount of time together since Genevieve's parents' divorce. Mrs Birch had taken on Gennie as her protégé. Gennie was what she called her. They'd spent an entire summer in the stifling non-air-conditioned music archives, cataloguing sheet music and archiving videos of the school concerts. And if you think sitting through one school concert is tough, try sitting through 138 of them! It's enough to make you tear your own ears off. **Oh, such lovely images.**

On certain days, when Genevieve's mum worked a second

shift, Gennie and Mrs Birch even ate dinner together. Always by the piano. They would sing and converse. They'd talk about french fries and butterflies and the things that mattered most, which often sounded like the things that mattered least. They seemed to laugh as much as they sang. And on one very special day, they cried. It was the day Mrs Birch shared the details of her own divorce and of the child of her own she could never have, due to a prolonged illness.

After Genevieve went home, Mrs Birch remained in the archives. She stayed all night, composing a sonata.

Yes, *that* sonata.

The next day, when Genevieve returned, Mrs Birch played the completed piece, and together they wept. Through song, Mrs Birch had summed up their special bond. It was funny and sad and sometimes silly. And like all true friendships, it transcended words. It was music.

She called it *Gennie's Friend*.

During the school week, Tobe's smear campaign continued in earnest. Genevieve, he had decided, wasn't a mouse at all. She was a snake. A jealous viper, and all the more dangerous for it.

Genevieve felt eyes glaring at her the moment she

stepped onto her bus. The students were bad enough, but no, not Wes! Yes, Tobe's smear campaign had reached Wes, the bus driver, too. By the time she got to class, Genevieve felt like an outsider in her own skin. And the online comments were even worse. How dare she question the integrity of the school superstar?

But the final nail in the piano came during rehearsals. By then, Genevieve was too upset to play, her eyes blinking out of control. Tobe had a hard time keeping the grin off his face. Her performance seemed like one giant mistake. Oh yes, the scholarship was a lock. Just one more turn of the screw for insurance purposes. That ought to do it.

It happened before lunch. Genevieve was called to the head teacher's office and told, in no uncertain terms, to stop bullying the young maestro. "*Me? I'm* not doing anything! Tobe stole Mrs Birch's music. And now he's bullying me!"

Mr Gribbons gave her a condescending double pat on the knee. "We don't make accusations we can't back up with proof."

"But I can. I *can* back it up!"

"So you have the proof? The original sheet music, perhaps? With Mrs Birch's name on it?"

Genevieve lowered her head. "No, I've never seen it. But… it's in the archives!"

"The archives are sealed."

"So let's open them," she logically suggested.

"Not until the police complete their investigation." Mr Gribbons opened the door leading to the hall. "There's really nothing left to discuss, Gennie."

"It's Genevieve. I'd rather you didn't call me Gennie."

"Very well… Genevieve. Good luck with the competition. I don't know if you've heard… Channel 12 News is coming. Bless that Tobe."

Genevieve swallowed her vomit, leaving the office in a blinking hurry. Several students had been waiting for her in the hall. From their paint-spattered clothes, she guessed they were from the Art Honour Society. Also, it said *Art Honour Society* on their hoodies. They chuckled with their hands over their mouths and parted to reveal their latest masterpiece. Taped to the wall was a painting of Genevieve, sitting at a piano, with her head turned completely round, facing backwards. The art teacher heard the commotion and emerged from her room, then tore down the painting. Too little, too late. The damage was done.

Genevieve ran straight for the exit. She ran and she ran,

never looking back. As Tobe watched her from the chorus room window, he basked in the glory, his victory complete. Now there was no one alive to stop him.

Poor Tobe, always concerned with the living when it's the dead he should be worried about.

He first heard it during registration. As usual, Tobe strutted in a few minutes late, the rest of the class assuming that was what geniuses did. The opening announcements had already begun, and Principal Gribbons's voice was booming over the PA. After the pledge, Principal Gribbons spoke about next Friday's competition and how their entire town would be watching. Every student was to be on their best behaviour. All heads turned towards Tobe as the resident musical genius made his way to his desk. The morning announcements were all about him; they usually were. But there was nothing usual about them that day. For just as Principal Gribbons was about to conclude, Tobe heard it – the opening notes of the sonata. The soft piano chords of the haunting melody lilted through his head and washed over him like a dream. Tobe sat up at full attention and looked around to see if anyone else had heard it. Was it being broadcast over the PA, or was Tobe just hearing things?

CHAPTER FOUR

"Did you — did you hear that?" Tobe asked of the girl next to him.

"Yeah," she responded. "We all have to wear black and white for the competition."

Tobe stared at her, then realised that she hadn't heard it. It was all in his head. The music was gone in an instant, so Tobe thought nothing of it. Oh, but he should have.

It was later, during third-period maths, when he heard the sonata's exposition once again. And once again, he assumed it was all in his head, since he had played the piece so many times. But this time, it sounded different. Like more of an echo. A sound shadow. Tobe closed his eyes and listened harder, giving it his full attention. And that was when he realised that someone – somewhere – was playing *Gennie's Friend*.

He opened his eyes and studied the faces of his fellow classmates. Most of them were struggling with Mrs Dee's triweekly maths quiz. Well, except for Craig Craft. He was struggling for bogeys, but that's a whole other story. And Mrs Dee herself, she was at her desk, scrolling through her phone. But the music was pretty loud. Why weren't they reacting?

Tobe got up from his desk and slowly walked towards the sound of the sonata. "Excuse me? Tobe?" It was Mrs

Dee. "We're in the middle of a quiz. Where do you think you're going?"

He didn't respond. Her voice no longer had a place inside his head. Tobe was entranced by the piano and the power of the sonata. It had overtaken his brain, gnawing away at his grey matter like a symphonic saprophyte.

"Tobe, are you still with us?"

It grew louder still. The haunting sonata was rising from an uncovered vent in the floor. Tobe got down on his knees and placed his ear against the metal grate. *That's it! It's coming from the basement. Of course. The archives!*

A petite hand tapped his shoulder, and Tobe turned with a start. Mrs Dee was staring down at him, her look moderately stern. One couldn't get too upset. After all, it was Tobe. "Would you mind returning to your desk?"

"Don't you hear it?" Tobe asked. No, make that *demanded*. "The piano. The sonata!" But almost as soon as the words left his mouth, the music ceased, as if the sonata was in on the joke.

Mrs Dee gave one of those condescending *poor baby* head tilts. "Are we feeling okay? Do we need to see the nurse?"

His classmates chortled. It was the first time Tobe had ever been laughed at. For the record, it didn't feel very good.

CHAPTER FOUR

"*We* are feeling fine!" cried Tobe. "But *you* need to get your ears checked, because you must be deaf if you didn't hear that!"

Mrs Dee turned to her class for confirmation. "Did anyone hear a piano?"

"No, Mrs Deeeeeeeeee!" the class answered in unison.

She turned back to Tobe. "Maybe *you* need to get your ears checked."

"My ears are twenty-twenty, Mrs Dee. I know what I heard!"

"This is maths, not music. And we're in the middle of a quiz. Won't you join us?"

Tobe shuffled back to his desk and, in the silent moments that followed, stared blankly at his quiz, the square root of 1,969 the last thing on his mind. He knew what he had heard and he knew what it meant. It was Genevieve's revenge. The mousy ones could be scary. They hid in corners, nibbling away at their cheese, waiting for just the right moment to unleash their telekinetic powers on an unsuspecting prom. Yes, it was her. It *had* to be. But why hadn't any of the other mice heard it? They must have. It was way too loud! Unless…

But of course! They were in on it, too. Yes, it all made sense. He'd been warned, hadn't he? By his third-grade piano teacher. The price of genius was the jealousy of others. But it would be a price worth paying. The talentless quiz takers were haters, too. They crawled out of the woodwork, like rats, first cousins of the mouse. And soon Tobe found himself doubled over with laughter. Having solved this little mystery, he laughed with relief.

Sure, the others stared at him. Why wouldn't they? *I'm laughing at you, quiz takers! You pathetic no-talents! Ace your little test, but remember: maths class never got anyone a standing ovation!*

It happened again during lunch. The sonata burst into Tobe's head just as he was taking a big gulp of milk, causing him to choke momentarily. The music seemed to be rising from the floor again, but no sooner did Tobe put his ear to the ground than the music stopped. Tobe gave the canteen the once-over. The no-talents just kept on munching away, but Tobe had had enough.

It was after his final lesson when Tobe ventured into the basement. He hadn't been down there since the first time he'd heard the sonata, back when Mrs Birch was still in the pink. He hadn't planned on stealing her music. Things just worked out that way. At the time, he'd been returning a stack of sheet

CHAPTER FOUR

music from the chorus room when he heard the opening. Truth be told, Mrs Birch wasn't the school's best pianist – he was – but her sonata was something special. It seemed to infiltrate his blood. The piece was sad and sweet and bitter and whimsical. A complete personality. But mostly, it was honest, something Tobe was not, nor would he ever be.

Tobe had been present when the music stopped – along with Mrs Birch's heart. It was on that fateful afternoon when he peeked into the archives. It was like a cave, loaded with compositions and vinyl records and CDs and instruments. In the centre stood Mrs Birch's piano… with Mrs Birch on the stool, frozen, like an ice sculpture. Her eyes were like glass, staring his way. And no, her head was *not* facing backwards. So much for canteen chit-chat. But she was definitely dead. They got that part right. Mrs Birch had died at her piano, her fingers touching the keys. She had told no one but Gennie of her lingering illness. And the sonata was a final gift to her young pupil and friend.

As you might have guessed, death wasn't the only thing that happened in the archives that day. There was a theft, too. Tobe saw the handwritten sonata on the music rack, and deciding it wouldn't do Mrs Birch much good, her being dead and all, he stuffed it into his backpack, careful not to touch the body or disturb any evidence. He'd seen enough forensics TV to know. But just as he was tiptoeing away, he heard a sound. It couldn't have been Mrs Birch, that was for sure. Maybe it was the wind. Everyone's always blaming voices on the wind. The wind should hire a lawyer and sue. But no. As much as he wanted to believe otherwise, it was not the wind. *CLINK*. It was a sound. A finger... striking a piano key.

Tobe ran. With the sonata snug in his backpack, he ran and never looked back.

He hadn't been down to the archives since that day, but in light of recent incidents, he decided to check it out.

And *that* was when the music started up again.

Tobe steeled himself as he headed down a long, dark stairwell where a single fluorescent light strip was sputtering, adding a movie-like strobe effect to his journey. He stopped when he saw the door at the far end of the corridor. It was wrapped in heavy chains, just like the chit-chatters said. He could hear his own heart ticking like a metronome, *thump-thump*ing to the sonata. Someone – **or something** – was playing Mrs Birch's piano on the other side of the door. The sonata suddenly grew much louder, too loud to be beautiful. Even though it was the same piece, it somehow sounded ugly.

Tobe covered his ears, trying to drown out the sound. He

still heard it, even as he backed up the stairs, tripping over his own two feet. "Stop it!" he shouted. "You're ruining it!"

With each step he took towards the door, the sonata built. "Stop it! Stop it! Stop it!"

Then a chill shot up Tobe's spine. He sensed a presence behind him, as if someone was watching him from the opposite side of the corridor. As the music reached its crescendo, Tobe turned round.

A shadowed figure was waiting for him at the top of the stairwell. It said nothing. Tobe screamed and the figure lunged forwards and grabbed his arm. Under the fluorescent light, Tobe saw that it was George, the caretaker, who hadn't been sent to a sanitarium after all. "What's all the racket about?"

"The piano!" cried Tobe. "Can't you hear it?"

The caretaker put a hand to his ear and listened. "I can't hear anything over the buzz of that fluorescent." He held up a replacement bulb.

But Tobe was insistent. "Someone's in the archives. You need to check it out. Do you have a key?"

The caretaker shook his head. "I do, but I can't. The archives have been a no-go since Mrs Birch... well, you know." He made a cut-your-throat gesture with his finger. "No one's in there, I can promise you that. And no one's supposed to be down here, either. Now get going or you'll miss the late bus."

Tobe remained a moment longer, staring suspiciously at caretaker George. "You're in on it, aren't you? I get it. You're just a caretaker. You're jealous. There are no standing ovations for mopping up vomit!" Tobe laughed right in George's face. In fact, he laughed so hard he didn't even hear the caretaker's retort. **Which is just as well, dear reader. The caretaker's retort was an adult locution not suitable for printing.**

The next day, as he was getting ready for his little cousin's birthday party, Tobe heard the sonata again. The piece swirled in from a TV set in the living room. It was being played in the background of a life insurance ad.

Life insurance. Tobe really should have looked into that.

Later in the day, he heard it again, this time at the party. Little Scotty had just turned six, and Tobe had bought him a toy piano as a gift. But little Scotty had no interest. He wanted the latest smartphone, not a toy for toddlers. Tobe was rightfully annoyed. Little Scotty was his blood relative; he should appreciate music just like his big cousin! In protest, Tobe chose not to sing "Happy Birthday" to the jealous little brat. Instead, he hid in the back of the games room while his relatives gathered round the ice cream cake. And that was when Tobe heard the toy piano. At first it sounded like someone banging on the keys, but then the music changed. **Oh, you know what it's about to play, don't you, dear reader?** The toy piano began to play the sonata, and chills once again performed their macabre melody up and down Tobe's spine. He approached the toy, terrified. It had been programmed to play kiddie stuff, like "Mary Had a Little Lamb", something like that. It couldn't possibly know *Gennie's Friend*!

So Tobe did what came naturally to the rationally deprived. He stomped on the toy piano. He stomped on it until it fell silent. Until everyone in the room fell silent. The jealous faces stared back at him, judging him. As if any of those idiots could pass judgement on a genius. Yes, Tobe decided, they were all in on it, all except for little Scotty. Because little Scotty wasn't staring; he was smiling. He hated the toy piano. "Now can I get a smartphone?"

Little Scotty didn't get his smartphone. And Tobe didn't get much sleep after that. Even his dreams were scored with the sonata. And when he opened his eyes, things got worse. The music was everywhere. He heard it on a car radio. From the landscaper's earbuds. From a girl whistling on the street. He even heard it being played as muzak at Food World.

Gennie's Friend was everywhere he was, and it was driving him mad.

Tobe was convinced 'they' were all in on it, including his mum, who he'd heard humming the tune during dinner. He couldn't believe it. His own mum, jealous! Just like Beethoven's mum! **Ahem. Beethoven's mother was never jealous. Just ask Beethoven. I have. We're old friends, you know.**

But they would not beat Tobe. He was determined to wow the world at the finals, which were now just one night away. He would win the scholarship on live TV and be hailed a genius. If only he could stop the sonata from eating away at his brain cells. A quick perusal of the hall cupboard did provide temporary relief. Tobe stuffed two handfuls of cotton wool into his ears. And it seemed to do the trick while also managing to block out every other sound on the planet, which suited him just fine. He didn't need to hear *their* words. He only needed to hear *their* applause.

But when he got to school, the sonata was waiting, seeping through the cotton wool like blood through a paper towel. Once again, a sour version of Mrs Birch's masterwork had risen from the archives. "I can still hear it!" cried Tobe as he tore the cotton wool from his ears.

Enough was enough. He was convinced that Genevieve had somehow masterminded everything, even though she hadn't been to school since the art incident. Or had she? She was a clever little mouse. It must have been her in the archives. But two could play at that concert. It was time to return to the scene of Mrs Birch's death – to break into the archives and discover the truth, once and for all.

That night, Tobe returned to the school with a pair of bolt cutters 'borrowed' from his neighbour's shed. He could hear the sonata rising from the basement and drifting out into the car park. He noticed that the gym door had been propped open, George the caretaker outside, grabbing some air. Tobe sneaked right by him and ventured down the stairwell, where a new fluorescent bulb was doing just as much sputtering as the old one.

The music was overpowering, and Tobe had to cover his ears just to keep his balance. "I can still hear it!" he cried. Soon it would all end and Tobe would know sweet silence once more.

The chain appeared to be rattling right along to the

music. *Can chains be jealous?* Tobe placed the bolt cutters on the lock's shackle and snipped it in half. The chain fell like limp spaghetti, and Tobe bravely swung open the door, announcing, "Gennie, I'm home!"

But Genevieve wasn't in the archives. Nor was anyone else. At least, not anyone he could see. What he did see, however, caused his eyes to bulge behind his fake glasses.

Mrs Birch's piano was playing on its own, unseen digits tinkling the ivories, the foot pedals pumping up and down. Gripped with terror, Tobe stared the way *they* stared at him. It *couldn't* be. It wasn't possible. But there it was, being what it couldn't. A spirit with an ear for music was playing the sonata.

This madness had to stop, and for once, Tobe had the means. He yanked open the lid of the piano and surveyed its innards, strings and hammers moving like the guts of a living organism, the composer's messenger.

"Shut up!" he shouted, but the piano would not listen. "Last warning!" The piano did not heed his command. It couldn't. Something else was in charge. So Tobe climbed in and got busy with the bolt cutters, surgically clipping every last string. *Snip! Snip! Snip! Snip!* The piano screeched in protest, crying out in a crescendo of high notes before growling its lowest lows. *Snip! Snip! Snip!* It continued to play. *Snip! Snip!* Now it was a simpler arrangement. *Snip! Snip!* Defiant to its very last chord, until all eighty-eight companions fell silent.

The task completed, Tobe climbed out of the piano and dropped to the floor, exhausted. The haunting sonata had finally ended. Perhaps he could get some sleep. He needed it, too. The next day was the competition. The TV cameras. The scholarship. The applause. He got to his feet, proud of his accomplishment and beaming with self-importance. If skill with bolt cutters deserved standing ovations, surely he'd have received one.

But he heard it again.

The piano had begun to play once more. *Impossible!* He'd cut the strings to ribbons. Had he missed a few? He turned and lifted the lid to check. If his ears had been playing tricks on him, his eyes would be another matter. Tobe peered into the piano in complete disbelief. Somehow, some way, the strings had repaired themselves. The keys and the pedals moved frantically, the haunting sonata echoing throughout the archives, growing louder and louder with each note.

He dropped the bolt cutters and covered his ears. It did nothing to muffle the now sinister sound. "I can still hear it!"

He ran from the school with his hands pressed over his ears. "I can still hear it!"

Tobe was last seen running through town, shouting at full lung capacity, some say singing in the melody of the sonata: "I can still hear it! I can still hear it! I can still hear it!"

The main hall was full. But the star of Buena Vista Middle School was a no-show. Most had heard the chit-chat concerning Tobe's mad exit the night before. Now the admirers were to gorge themselves on gossip, to fill the canteen coffers with something new, something awful. "I heard he went deaf!" "I heard he forgot how to play!" "I heard he ripped his own ears off!" Those were just some of the murmurings being bandied about before the curtains parted and Principal Gribbons made the formal announcement: Tobe would not be performing in the finals.

The crowd grew silent.

And after he departed the stage and the lights went down, a single spotlight focused on a figure seated at Mrs Birch's piano. It was Genevieve, wearing the best dress she could borrow. She lowered her delicate fingers onto the keys and began to play. She played the sonata as it had never been played before, with all the sweetness and sadness and whimsy that had come to define her. And she didn't blink once.

When it ended, there wasn't a dry eye in the house. None of the other competitors came close to her brilliance. The audience rose to their feet in a rapturous eleven-minute ovation that broke the Buena Vista Middle School record. And although certain individuals around these parts loathe a happy ending (Ahem!), Genevieve was awarded the full scholarship.

When the hall cleared, she remained on stage for a few minutes, soaking it all in. It was a night she'd only imagined. But amid her joy, there was an emptiness in her heart. If only Mrs Birch had been there. And for an instant, it was almost as if Mrs Birch was sitting on the piano stool next to Genevieve.

Oh, but she was. You see, occasionally the dead decide to right certain wrongs, and that's just what Mrs Birch did.

Genevieve smiled at the thought of Mrs Birch's sonata living on, yet at the same time, she also mourned the absence of her rival. Tobe was an egomaniacal bully, but she still respected his talent. Genevieve had performed magnificently that night. If only he could have been there to hear it.

She gave an exhausted sigh, regarded the piano one last

time, then grabbed her bag, ready to leave. And that was when she heard the clapping.

"Who's there?" She inched her feet to the edge of the stage. At the same time, a boy stepped into the centre aisle, silhouetted by a spotlight. It was Tobe – she could tell by his walk – but there was something different about him.

Still clapping, he emerged from the shadows, and when Genevieve saw him, she screamed a scream he could no longer hear. Tobe's ears had been removed. In their place were scabbed, crusty brown circles. Occasionally the chit-chat gets it right.

For Tobe, the concert hadn't ended. He had wanted the sonata, and now it was his. Forever. Mrs Birch's piano was once again playing the chords on its own, in an endless loop for all eternity. Tobe climbed onto the stage and extended his hands, presenting, as a gift to Genevieve, his ears, severed from his head. Genevieve looked at them, horrified, and continued to scream. Tobe looked to the piano and, in a voice reserved for the hopelessly insane, shouted at the top of his lungs:

"I CAN STILL HEAR IT!!!"

Chapter Five

THE NEFARIOUS NILE ROOM

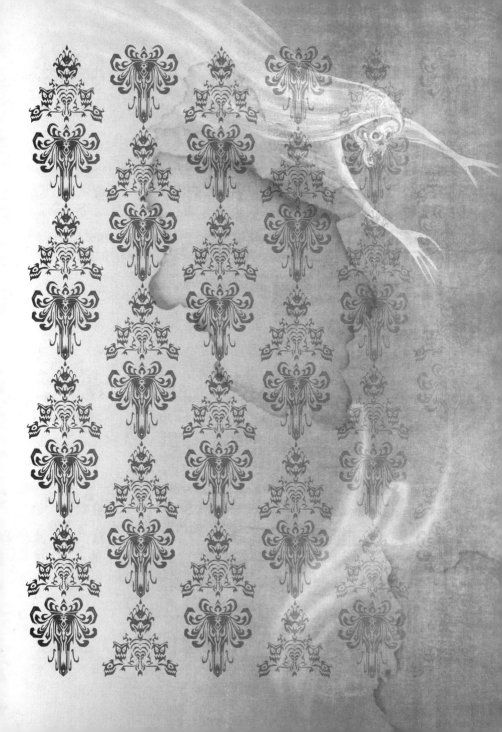

The piano was back where it belonged, the final refrains of the haunting sonata lingering like a sound shadow within the music room. The librarian slid his bony finger along the keys. "I can still hear it," he said with a sly grimace.

Marge and Pasquale remained suitably creeped out. And Declan remained suitably unimpressed. "Sorry. Music ain't my *ting*."

"Thing."

"That neither."

The librarian glided towards him, and Marge did a double take. Declan was at least a head taller, yet he and Amicus Arcane were standing eye to eye. "What is your thing, sir? Perhaps it's gold you desire?"

Marge nodded. "Seems he's got your number, Deck."

"My number's unlisted!"

The librarian made a sweeping gesture with his hand. "The mansion has *everything* you could possibly desire. Gold. Jewellery. Precious artefacts, considered priceless by most."

"You got a lot to learn, old-timer. Everyting's got a price."

On that, the librarian agreed. "So it does." There was a rumble. The threesome turned to see a panel opening in the wall, a secret passageway revealed. "If you'd care to follow me…"

"Follow you where?"

"Follow me there." The librarian pointed, tipping his candelabrum. Flickering candlelight illuminated the passage. The walls were glistening. And swelling. "If you would kindly transport the crate labelled 'Valley of the Kings'." Again, the librarian smiled. He looked worse when he smiled. He ducked his head and vanished in the passageway.

Marge turned to the others. "What do you tink?"

"There's 'art facts' down there. I tink **(think!)** we follow," said Declan. Pasquale thought differently. He was staring at the piano as if he'd just seen a ghost. (Or, more likely, heard one.)

Declan shouted directly in his face. "Yo! You comin'?" But Pasquale didn't answer the brute. He simply sat there. Staring. "What's with him?"

"The drive took a lot out of him," replied Marge, covering for her friend. "Maybe he should rest here for a while."

"Widdle baby needs a nap." Declan gave a contemptuous wave and headed off to retrieve the second crate.

Marge placed a hand on Pasquale's knee. "You gonna be okay, Pask?"

"This here's more than I bargained for," he finally responded. "Why'd you talk me into this?"

"Because. You needed the cash. You been dealt a bad hand lately."

He peered into her mismatched peepers. "Could be worse." And he smiled. "Forget the pay cheque. Let's get outta here while's we still can." He added in a whisper, "I'm worried about you, Marjorie."

Marge turned red (a slight improvement) before looking away. Strange how things turned out. No one had ever worried about her in the past. But on that night of all nights, in that place of all places, someone finally said the thing Marge had always wanted to hear: *I'm worried about you.* "I'm worried about you, Marjorie", to be precise. If you're bothering to quote someone, please get it right.

Marge backed away, fumbling past the antique furnishings. "I, uh, better go with him. If we ever wanna see the other half of that moola, ya know?" She scooted into the passageway, melting into the shadows.

Pasquale remained in the music room alone. Alone and upset. He should not have said what he'd said. He was there on business, and Marge was his partner. He just needed some time alone to think. Oh, but he was not alone.

A chilled air seemed to penetrate the enclosed chamber, moving with purpose throughout the music room. Pasquale lifted his head and watched as an indentation sunk into the cushion of the piano stool, as if an invisible someone had just sat down. And then, before his startled eyes, the piano keys began to move, accompanied by the foot pedals.

Pasquale had been joined by Gennie's friend.

Declan and Marge rolled the second crate into the Nile Room, where the librarian was waiting.

As the sobriquet suggested, the room contained

priceless treasures from an ancient world – pottery, gems and scrolls written on papyrus – handsomely displayed in a museum-quality setting. But curiously enough, there was no mummy. **Not yet, foolish reader, but if the dead can wait, then so can you...** A large rectangular display case stood empty. Perhaps the occupant was... occupied.

"Where is Master Pasquale?" enquired the librarian. "Has he departed... prematurely?"

Before Marge could answer, the rumble of stampeding footsteps shook the room. Something was fast approaching from the passageway. Declan raised his fists, ready to deal with it.

A figure flew in through the passage, ending up in Declan's arms. It was Pasquale, huffing and puffing, having left the music room in a hurry. "What's with you?" Declan demanded.

"I, um, just wanted to make sure you guys was okay," Pasquale said, looking at Marge.

"Yeah, sure we're okay. Look around!" Declan gestured about the treasure-filled chamber. "I'd say very okay!"

The librarian gave Pasquale a respectful nod. "I'm delighted you've chosen to rejoin us. Our tales demand to be heard."

"No more of your tales!" Declan snapped. "Unless they got gold in 'em."

"They do," replied the librarian, handing Declan the crowbar.

Pasquale joined Declan and Marge, and together they prised a wood-slatted cover from the crate and carelessly tossed it to the side. In the same moment, a dozen or more large lavender insects burst forth, crawling across their hands, nibbling at their fingers. A high-pitched squeal sent them scattering into hiding places throughout the room. It wasn't Declan and it wasn't Marge. And it certainly wasn't me! It was Pasquale, screaming out of control. Declan offered to smack him out of it, but Marge soothed him with a hug. "It's okay, kid. They're gone."

"Sorry about that," he managed to say with a sniffle. "I ain't big on roaches."

"Scarab beetles," said the librarian, politely correcting him. "Revered by the ancient Egyptians in days gone by." And we're not talking your parents' old days. We're talking thousands-of-years-ago old days.

The librarian glided backwards before addressing the trio. "If you will excuse me," he began, "I shall return momentarily." And with that, Amicus Arcane disappeared into the shadows.

Declan's mind was still on the scarabs. "Did you see those suckers?" Declan said, still in awe. "They was as big as my fist!"

"But not as big as *that*!" added Marge. She was staring wide-eyed into the crate, a bright orange hue reflected on her face. The others leant in to see. A golden sarcophagus, the ancient burial coffin of a prince, was resting peacefully within, moulded in the likeness of a pharaoh.

The threesome slowly lifted the sarcophagus out of the crate and placed it in its display case. It was heavier than it looked, and it looked pretty heavy. Pasquale and Marge stood, huffing and puffing, staring in awe at the ancient sarcophagus. Declan, on the other hand, looked the coffin up and down as a sinister smile moved across his lips.

"It's a mummy case!" shouted Pasquale.

Declan rubbed his hands together. "With rubies for eyes! Don't mind if I help me-self to some overtime." Declan looked around to make sure the coast was clear, then lifted the crowbar and quickly scooped out the eyes. Marge and Pasquale were mortified. As much as they needed the money, the sarcophagus was a historical work of art.

"That is most unwise, Master Declan." The librarian

had returned and was standing by a small tray, brewing up a concoction in a petite gold kettle.

"How did you—" Declan began before changing his query. "What's unwise, skinny?"

"The eyes, Master Declan. It would behove you to return them to the sarcophagus. Immediately."

"Why? They ain't doin' nobody any good in here."

"Those who steal from the ancients do so at their own peril," the librarian stated.

"Wh-what is that?" asked Pasquale nervously. "Some kind of curse?"

"I ain't big on curses, 'cept for the ones I say out loud," replied Declan, and he laughed – so hard, in fact, that he ended up coughing, thinking he was funnier than he actually was.

"The colonel did not believe in curses, either."

"Who's the colonel?" asked Pasquale.

"That would be Colonel Tusk." As soon as the librarian said the name, a scream-like whistle bellowed throughout the room. The threesome turned and saw steam rising from the kettle. The librarian lifted the handle and poured hot water into a cup through an ornate tea ball. At once, Declan recognised the lofty aroma.

"Is that…?"

CHAPTER FIVE

The librarian nodded. "Tusk's Tasty Tanis Tea."

Declan was instantly agitated. "Some moron told me they don't make it no more! When I get me hands on that guy..."

"That's right," said the librarian, "kill the messenger. Or don't kill the messenger. I never can get that right. The point is he was telling the truth. Tusk's Tanis is no longer available to those in the pink."

"Then how'd you get it?"

"We here at the mansion have... connections."

Declan no longer cared about the how. He reached for the cup, for a sip of the tea he'd been dreaming about for five long years. But the librarian moved past him. "This brew is not for you." He moved past Marge, too. "Or you." He moved past Pasquale, as well. "Or you." Amicus stopped by the head of the sarcophagus, where he knocked three times with his free hand. "It's teatime!"

The threesome watched, gobsmacked, as...

The lid *creeeeeeeeeak*ed open and a hand wrapped in mouldy linen reached out for the cup, looping a bony finger around the handle.

"You gotta be kiddin' me!" (Declan, of course.)

The lid slammed down, and from within the sarcophagus, there emerged an inhuman *sluuuuurp*. The librarian closed his eyes in wistful remembrance. "Ah, yes. The prince always did enjoy a cup of the old chai." He reached for volume three. And with the threesome staring in suspended silence, Amicus Arcane began a tale of ancient curses in faraway lands… and a long-dead prince with a hankering for tea.

Interlude

This is your second warning.

They are closer still.
You cannot see them.
You cannot hear them.
But they can see and hear you.
And not even the great sands of time can stop them.

You've been warned...

———— ✤ ————

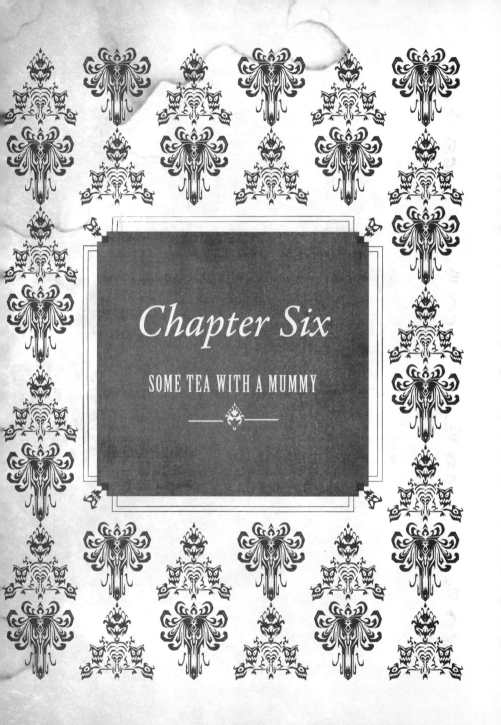

Chapter Six

SOME TEA WITH A MUMMY

Do you ever wonder why they took Tusk's Tasty Tanis Tea off the market? For a time, it was the best-selling tea in the country, if not the world – a national obsession, like Hula-Hoops and Pet Rocks and zombies.

You remember drinking it, don't you? Sure you do. You tried it. You liked it. It came in three fabulous flavours: Original Blend, Earl Grey and Bountiful Boysenberry. Then there were the TV adverts. The unforgettable jingle you couldn't get out of your head. The constant pop-up ads. The billboards plastered all over town, at train stations and on buses, featuring the product's unwitting mascot: an Egyptian mummy – dead for 3,500 years! – sitting upright in its sarcophagus and sipping a cup of tea.

And you might have enquired, *What in the world do Egyptian mummies have to do with tea?* A solid question. And one you might have asked before you sent away for that Tanis Tea Mummy plush toy you kept on your shelf… next to the Pet Rock. Still have it?

Pity. It's worth a fortune.

According to the packaging, Tusk's Tasty Tanis Tea was derived from the ancient tanis plant, thought to be extinct until an expedition uncovered a remarkably virile specimen under the sands of Egypt. The ancient Egyptians revered their beloved tanis plant for one simple reason: they believed that the tanis plant had the power to awaken the dead. Some of us are already up…

The Egyptians also believed that death was only the beginning, that our world was merely a stopover and that our spirits live on. And how right they were. The great pyramids were erected as tributes to the deceased. Their tombs were burial sites, intended to remain concealed for all eternity – very much like the burial sites of today. You wouldn't want some stranger digging up your favourite uncle, now, would you? It would be downright rude.

CHAPTER SIX

Not to mention exhausting.

As a deterrent, curses were often inscribed on the burial chamber walls, warning of a gruesome, horrible, unimaginable fate that would befall any intruder. What's the modern equivalent?

KEEP OUT!

But this being the twenty-first century, the belief in ancient curses – gruesome, horrible, unimaginable or otherwise – has long since perished under the unmerciful sands of time. And this brings us back to Tusk's Tasty Tanis Tea…

It was seven seasons ago when Colonel Bartholomew Tusk, the renowned exporter of world goods, led an expedition to the Valley of the Kings, Egypt, in hopes of uncovering some rare finds. He would not be the first to pillage an ancient land for profit, nor would he be the last. Had Tusk brushed up on his history, he would have known about the real-life fate visited upon the King Tut expedition of 1922, and the mysterious deaths that followed. But his interests were in the present, in the treasures he hoped awaited his party on the other side of that burial chamber wall.

The colonel centred his lantern, shining light on a series of hieroglyphs – the alphabet of the ancients, of which he had no knowledge – chiselled into the limestone. He motioned for his native foreman to interpret. "Any idea what this says?"

The foreman placed his finger under the symbols, moving left to right, then right to left. Hieroglyphs can be read in both directions. "From the seal, it would appear we have uncovered a royal tomb."

This pleased the colonel. "Excellent. Royalty usually means money. Go on."

The foreman continued. "The occupant died under mysterious circumstances. Possibly by assassination. He was… Prince Amenmose the Magnificent, betrothed to Princess Hatshepsut the Alluring; half brother of the boy prince Seth the Simple."

The foreman took a step back, and the colonel saw him shudder. An odd reaction. The tomb was anything but chilly. "There is a *curse*," explained the foreman. "A most terrible curse."

Colonel Tusk tsk-tsked the idea. "Curses generally are. Terrible, that is. That's what makes them curses." He pointed to one of the dig workers holding a pickaxe. "You, there! The chap in the back. Break it down!" The worker shook his head, muttering a response in Arabic. The colonel looked to his foreman. "What's he going on about?"

CHAPTER SIX

"He says hieroglyphs are a work of art. That the wall is irreplaceable."

"Really?" The colonel adjusted his glasses, taking a closer look. "Looks like a child's finger painting to me. I've seen better art on toilet walls." The worker made another remark. "What's he on about now?"

The foreman shook his head. "I would rather not say."

"If you value your pay cheque, you'll say."

That made things easier. "He said you are a fool, Colonel Tusk. An ignorant fool."

"Am I, now? We'll see about that. Read on!"

With the native workers bunched together like scared children, the foreman proceeded to interpret a warning from the ancient past. "'Beware! Go back! Madness and death await those who disturb the tomb of Prince Amenmose.'" He turned for the colonel's reaction.

"Oh, hogwash! There are no curses. And if there were, I'd wager three thousand-plus years has taken the nonsense out of this one." The colonel grabbed a pickaxe from one of the frightened workers and raised it, ready to strike. But a stranger's voice stopped him mid-swing.

"Curses exist for all eternity."

The colonel turned from the wall, readjusting his glasses. "Who said that? Come forward!"

A tall, dark stranger with a slender physique, wearing a black suit and a red fez, approached from the far end of the passage, affording Colonel Tusk a respectful bow. "My name is Bahgal, high priest of the city of Karnack. I beseech you, Colonel Tusk, stop what you are doing at once!"

"Are you with the government?"

"No. I work for" – the high priest hesitated – "a private concern."

"Well, then we've nothing more to discuss."

The colonel lifted the pickaxe again with one last comment: "We have a saying in the expedition business. The bigger the curse, the bigger the treasure." *Thwug!* He buried the pickaxe in the limestone – in the timeless work of art. *Thwug! Thwug! Thwug!* The workers, the foreman, the high priest all watched with their hearts in their mouths as the colonel pounded away – *Thwug! Thwug! Thwug!* – again and again, with flagrant disregard for their history. *And their curses.*

Within minutes, the wall was no longer a wall. In its place stood the circular entrance to a mummy's tomb.

—

CHAPTER SIX

Colonel Tusk was the first to enter the ancient burial chamber of Prince Amenmose. It was a short walk through a secret passage. Ancient tombs had a lot of secret passages. **Just like a certain mansion I know. Heh.** Torches and lanterns panned to and fro, barely penetrating the ancient soot that had remained undisturbed for eons. The colonel caught glimpses of the mummy's personal effects in the light of his lantern: beads, amulets, knives, arrows. And he wanted to see more. "Lights, please."

The foreman had just set up a spotlight on a tripod. He threw a switch, illuminating the chamber. The workers gasped.

The mummy's tomb was an architectural masterpiece of the ancient world, perfectly preserved, with great stone columns towering above their heads like California redwoods. On a stone platform in the centre, a golden sarcophagus **(yes, our golden sarcophagus)** had been resting untouched for over three thousand years.

The colonel approached, barely able to contain his excitement. He had to put his hands on it, to know the sarcophagus was real.

"Do not touch it!" shouted Bahgal. "It is the mummy's coffin. The prince is to be revered, not ridiculed."

"You're becoming a royal pain. Who's ridiculing? I'm merely admiring the old boy's bedroom set." Colonel Tusk slid his palm across the golden surface and a shock pulsed through his body. He yanked his hand away, blowing on his fingertips. "Strange. I felt something. Like a surge of electricity."

"Colonel, come quickly!" The foreman was calling out from the opposite side of the chamber.

The colonel made his way across, with Bahgal in tow. "What did you find?"

The foreman pointed to a sealed entrance that led to an antechamber. It, too, was covered with hieroglyphs. The colonel promptly asked, "Well, what's the story on that?"

This time, Bahgal did the interpreting, reading the ancient warnings aloud. "'Within this room rests the forbidden tanis leaf, whose power can awaken the dead. Those who enter do so at their own peril.'"

The colonel rolled his eyes. "Another curse, eh? This tomb's getting old hat." He ordered the seal be removed at once.

Seconds later, Tusk and his team were aiming their torches into an antechamber. It was one of several silos, stuffed to the brim with dried leaves. The colonel reached inside and collected a handful. "They don't appear to be very menacing. They look like tea leaves." He took a whiff. "Mmmmm. Delightful. Tanis, anyone?"

CHAPTER SIX

Bahgal clutched the colonel's arm. "Colonel Tusk, hear my words. Their purpose was to resurrect the dead. You must leave this place. Leave it exactly as you found it or suffer the consequences!"

"Thanks for the advice, old bean."

You can guess the next bit. This isn't volume one, after all. Colonel Tusk did *not* leave that place. He couldn't leave. He'd invested too much time, too much money. He instructed his crew: "I want everything packed and ready to fly in seventy-two hours. Including the old boy in the golden bed. While I'm waiting, I could do with a cup of tea."

"No, you mustn't!" the high priest shouted.

"Oh, I must."

The colonel wasn't worried about resurrecting the dead. His only concern was resurrecting his bank account. He could not leave Egypt empty-handed.

So as his team went to work boxing up the contents of the mummy's tomb, Colonel Tusk retreated to a luxury tent overlooking a palm tree oasis. And by the light of a desert moon, he brewed his very first cup of tanis tea. It took only one sip for him to utter the famous quote you've seen printed on the package: "This is the best tea ever brewed, and I've brewed tea all over the world!"

To the ardent observer, the gold relics of the tomb would have seemed the obvious treasures, and they were. But let's face it: museums across the globe are filled with relics. Colonel Tusk did not want to explain the rules or laws that he had broken obtaining them – but no one was going to question a bunch of dried leaves. And that was something he could work with. People were always looking for a new taste in designer beverages; so move over, mochaccino. Tanis tea was the hidden treasure Colonel Tusk had been searching for.

Tusk's Tasty Tanis Tea would make its first appearance in the States the following autumn. It was an instant success. But tanis tea also came with a curse, no extra charge. A curse that promised madness and death to those who defied the sacred tombs. And the harbinger of this curse would be the very marketing mascot Colonel Tusk had used to sell his brand around the world: a being no longer alive. A spirit as old as the pyramids, wrapped in moulded linens, reawakened to carry out an act of vengeance 3,500 years in the making.

Penny and Carter found themselves alone in a room with a dead man. They had purposely strayed from Ms Fisher's history class, but they weren't expecting the dead guy. They were stuck on a field trip and bored out of their skulls, so they'd begun searching for a more lively location, hopefully equipped with a vending machine or two.

They'd explored the dark corridors of the Museum of Ancient Antiquities before stumbling upon the Egyptian wing. The dead guy in question was a certain Prince Amenmose. A plaque above his golden sarcophagus read ON LOAN FROM THE COLONEL TUSK COLLECTION.

"Check it out!" Carter pointed through the glass display. "He still has his teeth."

Penny climbed onto the railing for a better view. It was true. Underneath the moulded linen, she could see inside the mummy's twisted mouth – a pained grimace, it would seem, harbouring a row of crooked, corn kernel-like dentures. The rest of the mummy's face would prove even less of a bargain. A thin layer of human rind, putrid grey, was tightly matted to its skull. The embalming skills of the ancient Egyptians were beyond reproach – remarkable even by today's standards. First they'd remove the internal organs of the deceased and place them in jars; then they'd bathe the body in secret preservatives and, finally, wrap it in linen. Without those skills, Prince Amenmose would be no more than a mound of dust. Just like your favourite uncle.

Penny hopped down from the railing. "Is this what you wanted to show me?" Carter shook his head. "What is it? Before Ms Fisher sends that weirdo Karl Freund to find us."

Carter dug in his pocket. At first he couldn't find what he was looking for, and a second of panic set in. Penny smiled at his awkwardness. She knew where the moment was going and waited, somewhat patiently, giving Carter his space. Finally, he came upon the item, snug inside a bubble gum wrapper. It was a plastic friendship ring, inexpensive but not cheap. "Penny, I—" He stopped, as if he'd forgotten the rest of the words. He hadn't forgotten the rest of the words.

Something he saw took Carter's words away.

Penny bobbed her head, trying to kick-start his spiel. "Go on. You wanted to ask me…"

But Carter couldn't go on. There was something behind Penny he couldn't take his eyes off of. And being that they were in the mummy room, Penny knew she'd better turn and see for herself. "What?"

She saw nothing – certainly not a living mummy in tattered bandages reaching out to grab her, which was what she'd half expected. **Oh, but there will be. Keep reading, foolish mortal.** In fact, there was nothing out of the ordinary, so she asked, "What in the world are you looking at?"

CHAPTER SIX

Carter pointed. "You. I'm looking at you!"

"What are you talking about?"

"I found them!" interrupted a whiny voice from the corridor. That weirdo Karl Freund was peeking into the mummy room, on direct orders from Ms Fisher. Of course everyone in school knew it was the day Carter would ask Penny to the middle school dance. Everyone including Penny. The only one without a proper clue seemed to be Carter, which Penny had found somewhat endearing. But the interruption startled him, and Carter dropped the ring. "You guys are in deep, dark trouble," Karl Freund continued, undeterred.

Penny grabbed Carter's hand, tearing him away from the sarcophagus. "Come on, let's get back before we get detention."

Off they went, Penny never seeing what Carter had been looking at. But Karl Freund saw it, and he was astonished, too. A giant mural had been transported from the mummy's tomb, depicting a scene from the past. It featured the prince's great love, the beautiful Princess Hatshepsut. And yes, you guessed it, the princess's face looked exactly like... Karl Freund's. No, wait, that's a misprint. It looked like Penny's. By all the powers of the almighty cliché, Princess Hatshepsut looked exactly like Penny!

Tusk's Tasty Tanis Tea hit the marketplace running. Talk about an instant sensation. Mochaccinos had gone the way of the pharaohs. Billboards went up, and the ads flooded the airwaves. And of course Colonel Tusk found the perfect mascot: a cartoon version of the mummy, the once-proud Prince Amenmose, sipping tea inside its sarcophagus. As a marketing tool, it was pure genius. But to the followers of the ancient past, it was an insult, punishable by madness and death and all the other unpleasantries curses are generally known to cause.

One such follower was the high priest Bahgal. The tanis tea craze was bad enough. But to see the image of a once-revered prince on toys and T-shirts and longboards… well, that was just too much for him to handle. So Bahgal hopped on the next red-eye to America, determined to put a stop to these unspeakable crimes against the ancients.

A taxi arrived at the Tusk estate just before dusk. And a massive house it was, too, with a full-size fountain featuring a stone likeness of the colonel himself wearing a pith helmet and matching safari outfit. A butler led Bahgal to the colonel's private sitting room, where he found the colonel, well, sitting – privately.

The colonel rose to his feet. "Bagel!"

"Bah-gal."

CHAPTER SIX

"Yes, of course." He extended his hand to shake.

Bahgal bowed respectfully. "You appear in good health, Colonel Tusk."

"Seems that silly old curse lost all its potency. So what brings you to this part of the world, my friend?"

"*You*, my friend."

The colonel jingled a gold service bell. Within seconds, the butler appeared in the double doors "Martin! Two cups of tanis. Original Blend."

"Very good, sir." The butler moved off.

"Not for me," said Bahgal. "The tanis plant was not cultivated for such a purpose."

Tusk shrugged. "Your loss." The colonel retreated to his chair – burgundy, like his smoking jacket. "Why did you really travel all this way?"

Bahgal hovered behind the chair. "Colonel Tusk," he began, "I've come to appeal to your better nature."

"I'm not so sure I have one. If it's to take Tusk's Tasty Tanis Tea off the market, I suggest you take the first flight back to Egypt." The butler returned, handing Tusk his cup of tanis. He took one sip. "Mmmm. The best tea ever brewed."

A violent impulse overtook Bahgal, and before he knew

what his right hand was doing, he had slapped the teacup out of the colonel's grasp, sending it crashing into the fireplace.

Tusk sprang to his feet. "How dare you!"

Bahgal clasped his hands, bowing his head in shame. "I apologise, Colonel. But I beg you to reconsider. I am here to plead with you to undo what you have done."

"Then you've wasted your time." Tusk turned away, refusing to humour the high priest any longer. The butler returned with a rag to clean up the mess. "Never mind that," barked the colonel. "Show Bagel to the door. He's overstayed his welcome."

"I know the way out."

Bahgal left the Tusk estate, anger brewing in his belly like tanis in a teapot. So the colonel didn't believe in ancient curses. He found them *silly*. But he would become a believer soon enough. They all would – *the hard way*. Bahgal was about to serve up a special batch all of his own. No, not Earl Grey or Bountiful Boysenberry or Original Blend. That night the high priest would be serving up a flavour known as...

Resurrection.

It was after hours at the museum, and all the patrons and workers had gone for the day.

Bahgal had remained after closing, hidden inside the caretaker's cupboard. He squeezed himself next to several mops and had to shove one foot into a basin to fit. It was tight in there, but these were the things he did for Egypt. When he was sure the night guard had fallen asleep – the snores were a dead giveaway – he carried a small thermos of tanis tea he'd purchased from World o' Coffee into the mummy room.

The mummy appeared to be resting most peacefully in its sarcophagus, its arms criss-crossed over its chest. Bahgal approached the glass case. *Rest while you can,* he thought. With the help of a glass cutter, Bahgal scored a hole so he could reach inside. Tanis was only part of the magic. He had to speak some ancient words, too. Bahgal removed a parchment from his jacket and read from the ancient scroll of life. **For your convenience, foolish reader, we have translated the words of the ancient text into modern English.** "By the leaf of the tanis, by the howl of the jackal, make supple his limbs, bring this mummy back-el." **It rhymed in the original language, so we thought we'd play along.**

Bahgal unscrewed the top of the thermos and carefully poured an entire twelve-ounce serving of tanis tea down the dried-out throat of the long-expired prince.

Bahgal watched and waited. He waited for more than

twenty minutes – anticipating the magic, the triumphant rebirth promised by the ancient words. But nothing happened. The mummy did not move. It never even wiggled a finger. Prince Amenmose was as dead as he'd ever been.

Had Bahgal messed up the ancient words? Was it the 'back-el' part? Or the tea – too sweet? Or maybe, just maybe, Colonel Tusk had been right all along. There were no curses. No secret spells. Tanis was simply tea – mind you, the best tea ever brewed, as per the quote, but just tea nonetheless.

Bahgal climbed down from the display, crushed by his own inadequacy. What would he tell the high priests back home? That the ancient scroll didn't work? That tanis tea was just a tasty hot beverage, popular at shopping malls? He ran his fingers through the hair beneath his fez. Lost in his thoughts, he backed into a gelatinous shape – a living blob standing right behind him! The high priest stiffened. Should he look? Should he turn? Well, he would have to, eventually. So he turned.

The blob in question was a belly – a rather large one – belonging to Terry, the night guard. "How'd you get in here?"

Bahgal attempted to explain: "Forgive me. I was admiring your mummy room and lost track of the time."

But the guard wasn't interested in excuses. His job was

to guard, not excuse. "You can tell it to the police!" And he lifted his phone to dial.

For Bahgal, things had gone from ho-hum to horrible in a hurry. He had failed in his evil high priest duties and was two seconds away from spending the night in a foreign prison – not to mention he was down the six bucks he'd shelled out for tanis tea, and it wasn't even a large.

"Let's go, pal!"

Bahgal began to follow the guard when...

The guard froze, his body stiffening as straight as a board, as if he'd just been zapped with 100,000 volts. His glasses shot off his face, and his feet slowly lifted off the floor, one, two, three inches.

What was happening?

Bahgal was smiling. Because he knew. **He knew just like you.**

He had spotted the fingers, wrapped in mouldy linen, clutching the guard's neck from behind. The tanis tea had done its job. The mummy was alive!

Bahgal looked on with both horror and pride. He had succeeded. He had resurrected a dead thing, an ancient abomination. But the guard was not the target. He was merely an infidel, a worthless distraction, not worth a second of Amenmose's 3,500 years.

"Release him!" the high priest commanded. "He is not the interloper."

The mummy seemed to understand, if not the words, then their intent. He flung his arm back, releasing the guard like an afterthought. The guard went airborne, sailing clear across the corridor into a prehistoric-world exhibit and landing, unconscious, on the back of a sabre-toothed tiger. The morning shift would have questions.

Bahgal craned his neck, staring in awe at the death-defying being towering above him – a seven-foot-tall chiselled mountain of decay. "Go now, Amenmose. Destroy the non-believer!"

The high priest's commands penetrated the mummy's finely preserved skull. The creature turned and shuffled towards the exit. He wasn't very fast. You'd most likely outrun him if you tried. But what the mummy lacked in agility, he made up for in supernatural ability. He was no longer a thing of the flesh. He was a spirit as old as civilisation, trapped within untold yards of linen. The shuffling of his footsteps was a whisper in the wind. He could see in the dark. He felt no pain. And he had a grip that could crush steel... or the throat of any victim he so chose. That night, the mummy had chosen...

CHAPTER SIX

Penny and Carter stepped out of the World o' Coffee onto the corner of Main and Anaheim, sipping their respective cups of Tasty Tanis, hoping to chase an unusual chill out of the night air. Naturally, Carter was hoping for a little more. As delicious as the beverage was – the best tea ever brewed, haven't you heard? – there were bigger things at stake on a night that had started like most but would end like so few.

Carter had retrieved the friendship ring from the museum's lost and found – he lost it, they found it – so he could finally make his move. He would start by telling Penny how he felt about her, for his was an infatuation that had spanned the semesters.

He had first noticed her in Ms Fisher's history class, second row, third desk from the whiteboard, where she sat, twirling her hair with a pen. There was something different about Penny's appearance, as if she belonged in another time. Maybe even another century. Penny was beautiful; that was true. But beyond her genetic gifts, there was something about Penny's manner. She commanded respect, even when she was silent. Her casual requests were obeyed without question, as if she was the queen of the middle school. Not that she acted that way. Penny didn't think of herself as anyone special.

Oh, but she was. It was in her blood.

GRIM GRINNING GHOSTS

It took Carter an entire month just to say hi. Two months later, he actually managed a complete sentence: "Was that the bell?" But when fate lent a hand, as it usually does in love stories – and ghost stories – Penny and Carter found themselves partnered up on a class project, researching the tombs of ancient Egypt. That had been three weeks earlier.

They walked in the cold night air, drinking their Tusk's Tasty Tanis Tea. Penny couldn't get enough of it. She said it made her feel like she was reborn. It seemed to make her smarter by the sip, and that night was no different. Penny began to expound on the ancient past as if she was speaking from experience. Carter was fascinated. "That's amazing! How do you know all that stuff? You don't look *that* old." He chuckled. But Penny didn't hear his joke. Her mind was elsewhere, shrouded in visions of a past world it wasn't possible to remember first-hand. Or was it?

"I see a man. A prince. He has slayed many just to be at my side."

Carter shuddered. "You're not talking about Will Hewitt, are you? Does he still want to beat me up?"

"No!" she replied, sounding lucid for a moment. "He hailed from a time since passed. The pharaoh had him punished for his crimes. Mummified! And buried alive!"

CHAPTER SIX

"Maybe you need to sit down," Carter suggested.

"His soul is awake! The mummy has returned from the world of the beyond to seek vengeance on those who would desecrate his tomb!"

Penny seemed trapped inside a nightmare, almost as if she was in a trance. Carter had always heard it was dangerous to wake someone from a dream, but Penny's words were starting to scare him, so he took the risk. He shook her and shouted, "Penny! Are you in there? Wake up! It's me! It's Carter!"

She blinked three times before awakening. **The third time's the harm, as they say.** At once, Carter could see the fog lifting from her eyes. Penny was back to normal.

"What happened?" she asked innocently.

"I don't know. You blanked out. You were saying some really strange things. I'd better take you home."

"No, I'll be okay," she insisted. "I'd like to finish my tea. Let's sit down in the gazebo." Carter looked across the lawn at the quaint wooden gazebo, the site of many first kisses, imagined or otherwise. At the moment, kissing Penny was the last thing on Carter's mind. Okay, so it wasn't the *last* thing on his mind, but it wasn't the first. The very first thing on his mind was her well-being. He truly cared about her – which, conveniently, is generally the direct path to a first kiss.

They walked arm in arm across the frosty grass, Penny looking to the stars as if the night sky carried a secret message only she could read. "You okay?" Carter asked. "What is it? What do you see?"

Penny lowered her eyes, once again meeting his. "The mummy," she replied. "He's coming."

Colonel Tusk was pacing across his sitting room, back and forth, back and forth. The colonel felt uneasy. It had begun with Bahgal. Very sensitive, those high priest chaps. Why was he still so angry? It was only a cup of tea. The colonel hadn't hurt anyone. He was a mostly honest businessman, and tanis tea had raked in an honest fortune, fair and square. If it hadn't been Tusk, it would have been one of his competitors. Lord Henry Mystic, perhaps. The colonel had got lucky. What was wrong with getting lucky every once in a while? He wasn't a bad guy. Hadn't he shared his good fortune with others? Hadn't he introduced the world to the best tea ever brewed?

He stopped pacing when he heard the sound of shuffling feet. The colonel clutched his heart as a shadowy figure appeared at the double doors. **Breathe easy, foolish reader, for it is not our mummy. Not yet, anyway...** "Will you require anything else this evening, sir?" asked his butler.

The colonel was relieved to see him. "No, no, no, that will be all, Martin."

"Very good, sir. Then I'll say goodnight."

"I'll say it, too. Goodnight!" His butler closed the set of doors, and the colonel chuckled. What had he expected? An ancient curse come to life? A living mummy? Silly. Preposterous! There were no ancient curses. Of that he was certain.

Returning to his favoured chair, the colonel decided a late-night read might calm his nerves. A short story would suffice. He reached for his bookshelf. Dickens? Hawthorne? Poe? Which friend would he visit with that night? Poe! Because the wind was howling and the flames in the fireplace had diminished. There was nothing better than a chilling tale on a chilly evening. Or any other type of evening, I dare say.

Town Square was situated 1.3 miles from Colonel Tusk's estate. The village was quaint by most standards, a throwback to simpler times – an old church on one end, a movie theatre called the Bijou, Rosie's Ice Cream Shop and, of course, the obligatory World o' Coffee. Please. How could there not be one? There's a World o' Coffee on every corner.

It was late. The shops were closed. The wind was acting up. And there was a monster afoot.

The dead thing in the rotting bandages shambled along the pavement, taking in the modern scenery. What sort of civilisation was this? Where were the palaces? The pyramids? And what of the stony surface below his feet? What powerful alchemy had hardened the desert sands?

The mummy crossed the main road, not at the lights. A city bus swerved to avoid running him over. The mummy watched the tail lights disappearing in the night. What strange chariots they drove.

Penny and Carter were sitting in the gazebo, taking sips from their respective to-go cups of tanis tea – Earl Grey for Penny, Bountiful Boysenberry for Carter – when the mummy lumbered past. The prince was on a mission, but the aroma of the tea made him stop cold. He recognised that smell. It was the life-giving tanis leaf. He turned towards the smell – towards Penny and Carter – and that was when he saw her face. She had the same striking eyes that had tamed a kingdom and conquered nations. It was the mummy's bride, Hatshepsut, reincarnated as Penny!

Forgoing his mission, Amenmose turned and moved purposefully towards the gazebo.

Penny saw him first – the soulless mass of moving decay. Then Carter turned and saw the lumbering figure moving towards them. He couldn't believe it – Penny's earlier rants had been true. The living mummy was coming for them! Carter nervously turned to Penny, and as he expected, she screamed. But it was a scream of a different sort. She screamed with adulation as she ran from the gazebo, as if she was greeting a rock star. "It's really you! The Tanis Tea Mummy!" Penny got in front of him and made a duck face, so Carter did what came naturally. He snapped innumerable selfies of himself, Penny and the Tanis Tea Mummy.

And that was all it took. After 3,500 years of yearning, the mummy was no longer in love with his princess.

He continued on.

Colonel Tusk had fallen asleep in his burgundy chair. The book slipped out of his hands. *Thump!* He opened his eyes. The room was almost glacial. He checked his pocket watch. Three a.m.

Tusk bent over to retrieve the book. He felt a presence and looked across the sitting room. There was an enormous shadow behind the curtained window. It couldn't be the butler. Too tall for Martin. Too tall for anyone! Tusk got up to investigate. He picked up a metal poker from the fireplace and held it defensively.

"Bagel? Is that you?"

He approached the window. "If this is supposed to scare me, you've failed. Miserably, I might add. I'll have you know I've tussled with alligators! Gone swimming with sharks! If you think a creaky old curse is going to do the trick, you're sadly mis —"

The colonel whipped open the curtains, and the imposing silhouette became a full-bodied vessel of horror! The mummy was staring down at the colonel from the porch. Tusk stumbled backwards, startled at first. And then, composing himself — after all, this man had swum with sharks! — he laughed. "Bravo, Bagel! Quite clever. A most ingenious costume. Don't tell me. Stilts? You've done my mascot proud."

The mummy's response was to thrust both arms through the window, shattering it. Broken glass rained down on the colonel. He now knew this *wasn't* a prank. The perpetrator had gone too far.

The colonel stumbled to the other side of the sitting room, but the mummy was in pursuit, each stride it took equal to three of Tusk's.

The colonel was backed against the wall, trapped. The mummy was directly above him, a towering monument, like a living sphinx. Tusk gripped the poker like a spear. "Stay back, I say! Stay back!" The mummy reached for the colonel with giant hands that could crush steel – and do worse to flesh.

"Stay back!"

The colonel shoved the poker directly into the mummy's belly. The ancient being felt nothing. The poker went straight through him and came out the other side. Tusk pulled the poker out and could see through the hole. The mummy was hollow. And the man who had tussled with alligators and swum with sharks could now add skewering a living mummy to his CV. He began to laugh again. Some say it was the moment his sanity ended and the madness began.

The colonel laughed…

… as the mummy approached his desk.

The colonel laughed…

… as the mummy reached for the teacup.

The colonel laughed…

… as the mummy slurped the last remaining drops of tanis tea from the cup, the liquid spilling over his shrivelled lips and down his dried wrappings. The colonel laughed and he laughed and he laughed.

You can still hear him laughing today. That's his throaty cackle echoing through the corridors of Shepperton Sanitarium, where the colonel permanently resides in a padded room, having traded his burgundy smoking jacket for a straitjacket.

"Ha-ha-ha-haaaaaaah!" Is he laughing?

Or is he screaming?

Postscript: Owing to the mysterious circumstances surrounding Colonel Tusk's condition, and as a result of the bankruptcy that followed, Tusk's Tasty Tanis Tea was permanently taken off the market. Once again, mochaccinos ruled the day. As for the present whereabouts of Prince Amenmose, the mummy vanished from the Museum of Ancient Antiquities without a trace. Some believe the remains were stolen by thieves. Others insist the mummy was returned to its tomb in the Valley of the Kings, where it remains dormant.

But we know better, don't we, foolish reader? The mummy currently resides in the old cemetery next to a gated mansion on a hill, sipping tea for all eternity... keeping his true history under wraps.

Chapter Seven

RESTLESS BONES ETHEREALISE

Amicus looked up from the book, having completed the second tale. "What is it they say about being doomed by history? Or is it *tombed* by history? I never can get that right." But Marge and Pasquale were not listening. They were already gone. **Fear not, foolish reader. They won't get far, try as they might. They never do.** There was only Declan, still contemplating the untold treasures that surrounded him.

"Where are the others, Master Declan?"

He shrugged. "They split. I guess your scare tactics musta done the trick."

"My… scare tactics?"

"Don't tink I don't know what you been up to." He gave an appreciative chuckle, one usually reserved for others of his ilk.

"And what would that be, Master Declan? What am I *up* to?"

Declan slipped the sarcophagus's ruby eyes into his pocket as he circled the room. "This whole set-up with the shipments from New Orleans Square. You been fencin' stolen property, ain't ya?" He chuckled some more as he surveyed the ancient relics. "And I can respect that, lie-berry man. Even the whole haunted house bit. A little cheesy, but it's the perfect cover for keepin' unwanted guests from stoppin' by, if ya get my meanin'."

The librarian smiled just a little too wide. "You certainly appear to have my number, Master Declan."

"Speakin' of numbers… I just revised mine. Show me your safe, lie-berry man."

"I beseech you, Master Declan," said the librarian with a benevolence to his tone. "Return the gemstones you have stolen while there's still time." He closed his eyes, picturing the alternative. "Otherwise… things might get messy."

"I already told you: show me your safe. I know you got one. Show me where it is or I'm gonna show you the hurt."

CHAPTER SEVEN

Declan slipped off his jacket, showing off his imposing physique.

And the librarian slipped off his face, showing off his true appearance. "I'm afraid there's nothing safe around here."

Declan Smythe had never been one to run away from a fight. Or a fright. But what he saw in the Nile Room was a vision beyond mortal comprehension. Normal human beings couldn't do what the librarian had done. At least, not live ones. Amicus Arcane had revealed the face of death – and it was the most terrifying vision of all. The horror that pulsated through Declan's bulging biceps made him forget all about the rubies and the treasures he'd hoped to find beyond the mansion's hidden passages and secret chambers.

So Declan Smythe ran. He ran through the nearest door he could find, emerging in the narrowest of corridors, where music from an unseen organist played and a floating candelabrum provided the sole source of light. He continued to run, passing portraits from which the wandering eyes of gorgons and cat people and vampires followed him as he tore by. He stumbled down a grand staircase, racing towards what he hoped would be the doorway out of that madhouse. But there were no doors. Just like there were no windows. And he soon realised that the very steps he'd been descending were actually heading upwards. Declan deposited himself in a domed attic, where he paused to catch his breath, huffing and puffing, both hands on his knees.

Declan hadn't noticed the many gifts and precious baubles that surrounded him. His mind, like his heart, was racing. He thought about calling out to his partners, but in all likelihood, the librarian had got to them, too. After all, Marge and Pasquale were the weak ones. Declan Smythe, on the other hand, was a survivor. The toughest tough in New Orleans Square. And once again, he was on his own. Or so he thought.

Declan was surrounded by 999 spirits who knew better. Spirits who understood the gifts he had squandered, and resented him for it. For he had squandered the most valuable treasure of all: life itself.

Declan sensed something moving towards him, an unseen presence. Was it the librarian? That creature that had removed its face? The old Declan would have tried to fight back. The one-eyed brute would have thrown the cadaverous old codger head first through the nearest wall. But the new Declan was literally shaking in his boots.

It was drifting closer, and Declan needed to hide. He looked around, trying to find a spot where he could disappear.

He reached for an old sheet to hide beneath and gasped when the sheet rose on its own. The single sheet turned into three, and they floated towards him. At first the spectres seemed to stare, and then they seemed to smile. As the song says, happy haunts materialise.

Declan ran once more. He went to the far corner of the attic and hid behind a large wardrobe. He pulled an old tarpaulin over himself and sank down low. And there he remained, for what felt like an eternity, holding his breath, as the chilled presence drew nearer, blowing through the attic.

Get outta here! Go bother someone else! But it did not obey his silent demands, and terror beyond terror, he could hear the contents of the attic moving, shifting. The thing was searching for him!

It called to Declan in an angel's voice, a voice that had once belonged to a woman. "Come out, come out, wherever you are!"

It didn't sound like Marge, although in his present state, Declan couldn't be sure. He wanted to call out to her, but he remained silent. Then he felt a waft of cold air blow past him. The spirit was close. Very close.

"Found you, my love," said the voice, and what remained of the old Declan toyed briefly with the idea of tackling the shapeless whatever-it-was. But the new Declan knew better. The new Declan could only wait, paralysed with fear, as something slowly slid down the tarpaulin to reveal itself to him. The ghostly figure of a bride hovered just above him. She was holding an axe. And when he saw the blade rise above the cap of her latticed veil, every hair on his oversized head turned as white as fresh snow.

Declan slapped his hands over his face, awaiting the blade's impact. But a blow was not forthcoming. The chilled air dispersed, giving way to the comforting sounds of a crackling fire. Declan lowered his hands. The maniacal bride was gone.

He was no longer trapped in the attic. He now found himself within the confines of a quaint chamber, being warmed by its hospitable fireplace. Could he trust what his good eye was showing him? The encompassing walls were lined, top to bottom, with old books of varying colours and conditions and marble busts on display. Declan Smythe had been transported to the mansion's library. But what of its resident librarian, the mysterious Amicus Arcane? Was *he* not the puppet master behind the entire shivery charade? It was time for Declan to find out.

Declan rose to his feet and called out, "Arcane! Come out

an' show yourself!" But his cries went unanswered. With no way out, he moved directly to the bookshelves, searching for an escape. Maybe one of the books was actually a lever that opened a secret passageway. After all, there were no exits, or at least none that he could see, and that always worked in the movies. Declan pulled out book after book, but there was no such secret passageway. Declan Smythe was trapped. So this would be his new prison; he would be surrounded by books instead of bars. The mere thought prompted the toughest tough in New Orleans Square to cry out, "HEEEEEEELP!"

And then, filled with panic, he frantically began pulling down the rest of the books from the shelves. Soon a pile built up at his feet. The stories mounted, one on top of the other, 999 tales in all… with room for one more. All that remained was a solitary volume, and Declan noticed that it was the same book the librarian had been reading earlier. Volume three stared back at him from a shelf, and Declan knew what it meant. He knew what had to be done.

He held the old tome in the palm of his oversized hand, squinting to focus with his one good eye. Declan didn't need to find the ending. The pages turned on their own, the ending finding him. And when the pages came to a stop, he read the final passage aloud:

"'The ancient being was merciless, especially to those who had mercilessly pillaged his tomb, exploiting his treasures and profaning his name.'"

When Declan completed the tale, the fire grew dim. Another presence had joined him in the library: the unusually large figure of a man, one that dwarfed Declan Smythe. It was accompanied by a scent he could well define. It was an earthly aroma from a world unvisited for 3,500 years. It was the smell of Tusk's Tasty Tanis Tea.

Declan Smythe turned to face his destiny. And the last voice Declan heard was that of Amicus Arcane: "Those who steal from the ancients do so at their own peril."

Marge and Pasquale were navigating through a long, narrow corridor of doors when they heard the cries. "That sounded like..."

"Master Declan..." offered the librarian, who now stood before them, wheeling the third and final crate on a dolly. He led them into the room at the end of the corridor.

"Wh-where is he?" asked Pasquale.

"As I was about to explain, Master Declan has chosen to skip our final tale." He alluded to the crate in his midst, the one marked *Salem, Mass.* "Would you mind lending me a hand? I'll return it, I promise. My own hands are not what they used to be." He held up his gloved hands, which had Marge and Pasquale guessing what was under the gloves.

Marge exchanged looks with Pasquale. Did they have a choice? It had become *painfully* evident that the mansion's librarian, this Amicus Arcane, had been in control of their fates from the very beginning.

As they began removing the lid, Pasquale felt something shift inside. "You feel that?" Marge leant her ear against the crate.

"Yeah. I heard something, too. It sounded like... breathin'."

Pasquale turned to face the librarian. "Who you got in there? Is it Declan?"

"Hades no! Master Declan is no longer with us."

"He left us here?" Pasquale looked at Marge. "That stinkin' rat!"

"Never mind him. Let's get this over with."

"Yes, shall we?" In the interest of time, the librarian lent a hand with the lid, without ever lifting a finger. He simply waved his hand, and the lid simply... moved. At the same time, Marge and Pasquale looked inside.

There was a handsomely crafted wooden door resting at the bottom of the crate. Resting... literally.

"It's just a door!" said Pasquale, momentarily relieved.

"Oh, but it's so much more." The librarian was beaming with parental pride. "Fully handcrafted from the finest oak imaginable. Or is it *un*imaginable?"

Marge was instantly taken by the door's sculpted beauty and ornate handle, which resembled a curved snake. She reached to touch its face. "Ow!" She quickly retracted her hand. "The handle. It tried to bite me!"

The librarian gave the door a disapproving leer. "Now, now! Mistress Marjorie is our guest." He held up volume three, now back in his possession. "You would, perhaps, be interested in hearing how her story unfolds?" He wasn't asking; that they knew. The librarian opened the book and, with Marge and Pasquale his unwitting audience, began to read our third and final tale.

Interlude

We have arrived at your third and final warning.

Just as the young protagonist of our next tale will discover,
not all is as it seems.
As it was then, so it is now.
"As the moon climbs high o'er the dead oak tree,
spooks arrive for the midnight spree..."

Beware.

———— ❦ ————

Chapter Eight

THE DOOR THAT BREATHES

Ellen was blindly following orders, and blindly following orders usually leads to trouble. She had been instructed – the parental euphemism for ordered – to find the tallest, healthiest tree in the woods and report back home, pronto! Her father was a professional carpenter, you see. He sold premium wood furnishings for a living. You might know him from his advert. "Come on down to Big Ed's Discount Furniture, where the deals are real and the wood is good."

All right, so Big Ed was a carpenter, not a poet.

He'd started Big Ed's Discount Furniture out of his garage,

when he and Ellen's mum were still newlyweds. It took some time for the business to percolate – three long years (everything comes in threes) – but when his big break finally came, Big Ed had more work than he could handle. Quality was the key. He took pride in his craft. Big Ed hailed from a long line of carpenters. His great-great-great-grand-something-or-other supposedly lathed the mast on the *Mayflower*. At least that was what the story on Big Ed's website said. Was it true? Who knew? No one had ever bothered to look it up. Customers don't want history lessons; they want chunky armoires with ample drawer space. And they want them for a price.

"Come on down! The wood is good!"

So Ellen was assigned the task of venturing into the woods and finding raw materials. That meant good wood. Trees. The fatter, the better. Sort of like Ellen's dad.

She had a late start, having stayed after school to audition for the autumn play. That year they were doing *The Crucible*, a show about hysteria sweeping through a small town in 1692. The play was famous the world over. It told the story of a clique of teenage girls who accused their neighbours of consorting with the devil. And get this: it was based on actual history. It really happened. But what made it more compelling, at least to Ellen, was where the events took place: in her home town.

Ellen was born and raised in Salem, Massachusetts.

And if you don't know what Salem's famous for, don't ask Big Ed. He'd tell you they're famous for premium wood furnishings, and he'd only be half wrong.

Salem is famous for witches.

The sun had begun to set on the fabled woods, where tales of witches and warlocks were as commonplace as those of Cinderella and Peter Pan. The path was difficult, changing from patchy grass to prickly bramble in a few short steps. There was something other-worldly about the Salem woods, in particular. About the snakes and the owls and the frogs. The same wildlife that had served the witches of legend, the ones we still talk about, not in whispers but in our best projected stage voices. The hysteria. The trials. The hangings. It all happened there.

Ellen had always been a brave sort, though not by choice – at least, not a conscious one. No one ever decides to be brave. You're either born with it or you're not. Of course, it bothered her that her smartphone was down to a measly three per cent. **Because everything comes in... percentages?** It was two weeks before Halloween, not the best time to get lost in the woods. She had used up most of her battery documenting her hike. Now she couldn't even make an outgoing call. Forget the maps app! Not that she needed confirmation. Ellen knew exactly where she was.

Ellen was in the last place she wanted to be: the middle of the creepy old woods at sundown.

She hoped her phone wouldn't supply the impetus for a found-footage horror movie in which she was the star.

Calling upon her Girl Scout skills, she located the last shafts of the setting sun. *West,* she reminded herself. *The sun rises in the east and sets in the west.* That would have been an enormous help had she known which direction she'd come in from. The best thing she could do was turn round and hope to find her way back. But with the light almost a memory and overhanging branches closing in like Mother Nature's umbrella, Ellen's sense of hope had begun to fade. **We said she was brave; we never said she was an optimist.** She was honest-to-goodness lost.

The darkness was upon her now, and with it came those woodsy sounds that emerge in the night. The ones she could identify were fine. Crickets: good. Croaking toads: not bad.

CHAPTER EIGHT

A rustling in the trees: acceptable. Nearby footsteps? Bad. *Really* bad.

Nearby footsteps were gulp-worthy.

Ellen heard twigs snapping. Someone else was in the woods. For Ellen, this was a case of good news/bad news. The good news: she was no longer alone in the woods. The bad news: she was no longer alone in the woods!

She squatted like a toad, hopping behind a thick berry bush. The footsteps were coming from the other side. They weren't animal; she could tell from the pattern. They belonged to people moving in a circle. Her curiosity piqued, Ellen separated the branches. What she saw forever changed her world.

Three slender figures were moving round a small altar of lighted candles and gold chalices erected on the forest floor. They wore loose-fitting robes, all black, with large hoods hiding their faces; their feet were bare. Ellen had read about this sort of thing. It was a secret ritual. And for some reason, it didn't scare her in the least. On the contrary, Ellen felt oddly warm and invigorated.

The figures stopped circling, holding their positions. Had Ellen been spotted? The tallest of the three lowered her hood. She was a young woman with fiery red hair, just like Ellen's, breathtakingly beautiful – in her early twenties, Ellen guessed. The redhead motioned with her hands, and the others' hoods came down, too, revealing a blonde and a brunette. They could have passed for sisters, one more glamorous than the other. They shared the same Celtic features, the same glowing eyes, like a cat's, with a natural assist from the bright autumn moon. The redhead raised her arms to the heavens and spoke the words of ancient tradition. "By earth, by sky, by sea, as I do will, so mote it be."

The young ladies clasped hands, their energies combined, the redhead calling forth the natural forces. Her words echoed, as if they were being pumped through a loudspeaker – without a microphone, mind you. She would have clinched the lead in the play. Strong winds whistled through the trees and took down branches, yet through it all, the candles never lost their flames.

It was the most exhilarating moment of Ellen's life. She had to capture it. Without proof, who would ever believe it? She lifted her phone, the battery down to a pathetic two per cent. Still, it would be enough for a single selfie, with the mysterious beauties holding hands in the background. That was all the proof she'd need.

CHAPTER EIGHT

Ellen turned her back to the clearing and lifted her phone. *Click.* The shot went off – no flash, thank you very much – then it was back to crouching-toad mode.

Suddenly, the woods fell silent. It was like the entire universe had switched to mute.

Ellen looked at her screen. You must always look before sharing, kiddies. There she was, leaning in from the left side. Perfecto. But what about the young ladies? The clearing was empty. In their place stood a magnificent oak tree, its branches extending into the wilds like arteries, the embodiment of life itself.

Big Ed glanced up at an oversized wooden clock on the showroom wall (retail price $169.99, twenty per cent off if you became a Big Ed member). It was almost nine and he hadn't heard a peep from Ellen. It wasn't like her not to call or text. That was his number one rule, another parental term for you-know-what: if you're running late, call or text. It was mandatory.

He tossed his wooden key ring to the assistant manager... Woody. "You mind locking up? I've got to go read my daughter the riot act."

—

It was cold, it was dark and the time had come for her teeth to start chattering. Still, Ellen had to investigate. She stepped out into the clearing and almost had a heart attack when she saw them. The young ladies were standing in the same positions, as if they hadn't moved.

"Hello," said the redhead.

"I'm sorry. I didn't mean to interrupt. I'm kind of lost, and my stupid phone's on zero."

"Check again," said the brunette.

"Excuse me?"

"Your phone. Check the battery."

Ellen shook her head. "Trust me, I checked it like ten times already." She checked anyway, just to humour the young lady. Ellen's mouth dropped open. The battery icon was filling to one hundred per cent. "How in the world did you do that?"

"I didn't," replied the brunette. "You did."

"You can do anything you set your mind to," added the blonde.

The redhead smiled, seeing the confused look on Ellen's face. It was all too much for her. "I know. That sounded like something your mother might say."

"My mother is dead," responded Ellen.

CHAPTER EIGHT

The redhead nodded. "Which explains your natural gifts. Learn to trust your instincts. They'll never steer you wrong."

The young ladies began gathering their ceremonial supplies, loading them into hiking backpacks. Ellen had a question for them before they left. It was a biggie. "Can I ask you something?"

"Of course," said the redhead, smiling.

"You guys wouldn't happen to be..." She stopped herself, the sentence seeming too silly to complete.

"Witches?" said the redhead. "Yes. As a matter of fact, we are."

"But you're so... beautiful."

The young ladies laughed. "You were expecting green hags, soaring across the full moon on their broomsticks?" said the brunette.

"Well, yeah, sort of."

"We have those, too," said the redhead. "Witches come in all shapes and denominations."

"Although we prefer the term *naturalists*," added the blonde. "It's more palatable to the public at large. Unfortunately, certain prejudices still exist."

"Like in *The Crucible*," said Ellen.

"Like in *The Crucible*."

Just then, Ellen remembered her father. It was thirty minutes past her curfew. "Oh no, my father's going to kill me!" She swiped her screen, turning her phone into a GPS.

Again, the young ladies smiled. "You don't need a map," said the redhead.

"Trust me, I do."

"Trust yourself. Cats find their way home all the time, and they don't have a GPS."

"Yeah, well, the problem is I'm not a cat."

"Just close your eyes," said the redhead, "and visualise a path out of the woods."

"Right. I'll just use the Force."

In response, the redhead bowed her head and calmly repeated herself. "Just close your eyes and visualise a path out of the woods."

"Okay. I'll give it a shot." Ellen switched off her phone and closed her eyes, imagining a path – the most direct route home. And within a few seconds, she actually saw it – a path out of the woods, glowing electric blue. When Ellen opened her eyes, the blue haze faded, but the path was still there. The young ladies smiled.

"Bright blessings," said the redhead.

"Goodnight," said Ellen. She instinctively, unconsciously

removed her shoes and, walking barefoot, followed the path out of the woods, no longer lost.

Big Ed waited until the next morning to read his daughter the full riot act. During breakfast, he reminded Ellen about the rules. "You broke numero uno, missy. Text or call. That's going to cost you your phone for a week."

"I sent a text." She flashed a smile, the same as the redhead's. "Check your phone."

Big Ed had checked about a hundred times the previous night, and there had been no text. But when he looked at it that morning, sure enough, there was a text from Ellen. Big Ed shook his head in confusion. "This doesn't make a lick of sense."

"Does it ever?"

Big Ed glared at his daughter, not happy with her tone. "What was it you said there?"

"Nothing. Never mind." She took a bite of her blueberry pancakes. "You wouldn't hear me anyway."

Big Ed crossed his eyes, which meant he was angry. Confused and angry. "Was that a slight about my hearing? I work with power tools. Hearing issues come with the territory." He thought about pounding the oak table (special value price: $799.99). "What's really on your mind there, Elle? I've been getting this weird vibe out of you since your birthday."

Ellen did have something on her mind. And if she was brave enough to think it, she ought to be brave enough to say it. "It's just... if you were so worried about me, then why'd you send me into the woods in the first place?"

"Why'd I *what*?" Big Ed might have been good with his hands, but a deep thinker he was not. It wasn't easy being a single dad under normal circumstances. But being the dad of such a headstrong girl – one as headstrong as her mother – posed special challenges. "You've gone looking for raw materials dozens of times. I don't know why last night was any different." But Ellen did. **As do you, dear reader.**

Ellen ingested some more pancake, saying nothing, hoping he'd drop it. Big Ed took hold of her phone and started scrolling through her pictures. His eyes turned into Os when he saw it. "*Ho*-ly!" It was the shot of the magnificent oak tree. Ellen slapped her forehead. Why hadn't she deleted it? "Great work, Elle. You're out of the doghouse. For now." Big Ed stuck his fork in Ellen's pancakes, helping her out with breakfast. "I just need to stop by the shop before we go."

"The shop? What for?"

CHAPTER EIGHT

"Mr Do-Right. You can't have a party in the woods without him." Ellen's heart sank. Mr Do-Right was what her father called his turbo advanced dual-action chainsaw. He took another look at the tree – the brawny stump, the sinewy limbs – and smiled with begrudging admiration. The old trees were the toughest. "Yessiree, this old-timer's going to put up a fight!"

But Ellen had a hunch there was something more. Call it instinct. A premonition. Ellen was scared for both of them.

Try as she might, Ellen couldn't talk Big Ed out of returning to the woods. He was nothing if not pig-headed. Her mother used to call him that. A wise woman, Ellen's mum.

The witches' clearing looked peaceful in the light of day. A private sanctuary, where one might go to meditate and become one with nature. "Isn't it special, Pop?"

"It's a good space," replied Big Ed, and Ellen hoped, just maybe, he'd had a change of heart. "Once that tree comes down, it'll be a great spot for a barbecue pit." Never mind. She had to go with a more direct approach.

"Can't we just leave it the way we found it?"

"Sorry, sweetie. This here tree means too much to the store. She's gotta come down."

He steadied the chainsaw in front of his chest and yanked on the start-up cord. Mr Do-Right coughed up a little petrol. Big Ed pulled again. *Cough-cough.* "Wakey-wakey, Mr Do-Right. Third time's the charm!" Yes, Big Ed knew that one, too. He was about to pull the cord a third time when a voice called to him from the trees. It sounded somehow familiar. Almost like the voice of his late wife.

"Please reconsider."

He lowered the chainsaw and looked around. "Tara?" That was her name. Of course it couldn't be Big Ed's wife. She had passed. "Who's there?" A bevy of doves exploded from the trees.

In the same moment, a set of branches parted on their own and the young redhead entered the clearing. She was dressed casually in jeans and a tunic top, her hair tied back in a ponytail, her feet still bare. In the light of day, she was a fresh-faced college kid. "Hello, Ellen. It's wonderful to see you again."

"You too." They exchanged knowing glances. What they *knew* remains a secret between girls. "This is my father."

The redhead recognised him from his ads. "Big Ed."

Big Ed took a bow, the biggest celeb in town. But there are no standing ovations for premium furniture makers. "And you are?"

CHAPTER EIGHT

"Abigail," said the redhead. "I met your daughter last night."

"Is that right?" He turned to Ellen. "Funny. She never mentioned it."

"It never came up!"

The redhead levelled her eyes at the chainsaw. "May I ask what you're going to do with that?"

Big Ed spun the tool by its handle, as if he was some kind of lumberjack ninja. "Mr Do-Right has an appointment with a tree." And with that, he gave the start-up cord a third and final yank.

Brrrrrrrruuuuuummm!

The chainsaw was awake and ready to party.

The redhead put up her hand in protest. "Oh no, you couldn't! You don't understand. That tree has stood watch on this land for over a thousand years, since before the Pilgrims landed."

On a ship with a mast whittled by my great-great-great-grand-whatever-he-was, thought Big Ed. "That so? You own it?"

"No," she replied.

"And neither do you," added Ellen.

"Hey! Whose side are you on?" He brought Mr Do-Right's

motor down to a steady purr. "It so happens I have all the permission I need." And that was true. He'd given the mayor a sweet deal on some bedroom furniture, meaning Big Ed could cut down whatever tree he wanted.

Tears welled in the redhead's eyes. "Maybe you have a legal right. But there's more than legality at stake. We're talking about a very old soul."

"We're talking about a tree!"

"Please, Pop! Just listen."

Listening wasn't Big Ed's strong suit. But Ellen seemed genuinely concerned, and he was trying to be a more sensitive dad, so he retracted the chainsaw long enough to hear what Ellen's new friend had to say. "Thirty seconds. Impress me."

Ellen made eye contact with the redheaded beauty. *Talk fast!* The redhead pleaded her case. "This magnificent oak is more than a tree. The Puritans hanged witches from her branches." She made a sweeping gesture with her hand. "This is now our place of worship. We call it a nemeton."

Big Ed wrinkled his forehead, confused, and in only half the allotted time. What was this hippie talking about? The woods weren't a place of worship. They were a place for hiking and camping. And the Puritans! That was ancient history. Who cared about history?

CHAPTER EIGHT

"Sorry, snowflake. You'll just have to find yourself another tree to name. This one's got 'Mr Do-Right' written all over it." He revved the chainsaw, full power. *Brrrrrrummm! Brrrrrrummm!* A mechanical roar invaded the halcyon world. The birds, the toads, the crickets all fled. Mr Do-Right was a monster to be feared.

"Chaaaaarge!" Big Ed squared off with the oak in a duel to the finish. He tucked in his elbows and thrust forwards with the cutting chain. But before he could strike the first blow, the redhead stepped in front of the tree – so fast, in fact, that Big Ed almost didn't see it happen. "Are you crazy?" He lowered the chainsaw. "I could have split you in two!"

"Then why didn't you?"

Big Ed upgraded his look to *super* confused. "Is that a trick question? Do you think I'm a killer?"

"You were about to kill that tree," replied the redhead, referencing the mighty oak. "And she's a living being, too, older and wiser than you or I. With a past worth remembering." She stroked the trunk. "To my people, this tree is sacred."

"And to my people, she's a table and six chairs," replied Big Ed. "Now step aside before you get hurt."

Abigail's eyes grew wide as Big Ed moved past her and

went to work, stabbing and carving into the defenceless oak, its branches dropping like severed limbs, sap spraying his plaid shirt in blood-like geysers.

"Noooooooo!" The redhead watched with profound sadness. She wept, not only for the dying tree but for the death of a father's heart, a man whose own brand of morality mattered more than the pleas of his loving daughter. And in that moment, something magical occurred. The redhead became one with the tree, reacting to every blow, sharing its pain, its undignified end.

Ellen cried out. "Stop it! Pop! You're killing her!"

But Big Ed didn't hear a word. Mr Do-Right was drowning out all other sounds. And people like Big Ed never really hear what they don't want to hear, anyway. So he continued his assault, carving and slicing until the tree collapsed a few feet from the redhead. And as the tree fell to the ground with a mighty crash, Abigail fell to the ground with a laboured wheeze, struggling for air. Only then, wiping sawdust from his face like a soldier awash in the blood of a fallen enemy, did Big Ed see the shattered look on his daughter's face. Ellen was cradling the redhead in her lap, rocking her, trying to visualise a heartbeat.

But that was a magic she did not possess.

CHAPTER EIGHT

No charges were filed. In fact, there wasn't even an inquiry. The young woman, it was decided, had died the way she had lived: naturally.

But Ellen felt differently. In her court, Big Ed was guilty. And in the days leading up to Halloween, she kept her dealings with him to a minimum, giving him one-word answers mostly: yes, no, maybe. And Big Ed sure was feeling it. He felt as guilty as sin.

"How's the school play coming along?"

"Yes. No. Maybe."

He hadn't intended for it to happen. And the sensitive-dad books didn't have the answers, not for *that* one. Big Ed had to do something. He'd have to get his hands dirty on this, to prove to Ellen that he had a heart after all.

For three straight days, he laboured through the night, guided by an unknowable force. The ornate details, the intricate carvings, it was of a calibre beyond his talents. What Big Ed had been working on was anyone's guess. Go ahead. You're anyone. Take a guess.

And in seventy-two hours, it was finished. A beautifully crafted wooden door, forged from the remains of the magnificent oak. Excellent work, Master Edward. A door made from a hanging tree. What could possibly go wrong? Heh-heh.

Ellen couldn't shake the sadness, her heart feeling emptier than it had in years. After play rehearsal, she went directly to her room and threw herself face down on her bed. She thought a power nap might help her forget. But it didn't. The death of her redheaded friend, a person she'd known for all of ten minutes, felt like the most profound loss since the death of her mother.

"Ellen."

She mushed her face into her pillow. "Ellen!" someone cried out. She'd heard that; she was sure of it. It was a familiar voice. Could it have been Abigail? Was that even possible? Ellen sat up to look.

She did not see a redheaded beauty standing at the foot of her bed. What she did see made her feel decidedly worse. In fact, she was infuriated.

The wooden door, hand carved from the mighty oak by her father, was staring back at her, having replaced her old wardrobe door. It was a superior piece of craftsmanship – she'd give her dad that – but so what? The tree had also been a masterpiece.

Big Ed was relaxing on his Big Ed recliner (retail price: $599.00) when Ellen stormed into the living room, unannounced. "I want that thing out of my room! Immediately!"

Big Ed did a double take; that was how much his daughter resembled his late wife. "You've seen the door. Lovely, isn't it? If I may say so myself."

"Was it the tree?" Big Ed didn't want to answer. He could tell from her tone whatever he said would come out wrong. "Answer the question, Pop."

"Yes. It's the tree. I thought it would make you happy."

"Well, you thought wrong."

Big Ed threw up his hands in defeat. "I give up. I can't win for losing around here!"

"It's not about winning or losing! That wasn't a regular tree. It was a hanging tree."

"It looked like a regular oak to me."

"It's local history, Pop. *Our* history! They hanged witches from that tree. And the Puritans who crossed those witches, they all died horribly!" Ah, horribly. It's the only way to go!

But Big Ed wasn't buying it. "There are no such things as witches. They're superstition, like dinosaurs and low-fat desserts."

"It's fact! It happened here. Right here in our village! The girl who died, her name was Abigail. She was a good witch! She tried to warn us."

Big Ed was losing his patience. "I said I was sorry. It was an accident. How many times do I have to say it?"

"You want an exact number?"

"I don't like your attitude!"

"I don't like yours, either!"

"You're sounding more and more like your mother by the day!"

"Thank you!"

"You're *not* welcome!" Big Ed jumped up from his chair, a full head taller than Ellen, as he was most people. "What's got into you? You used to be the bravest girl I knew. Now you're afraid a door's going to get you?"

"No." Ellen took a breath and added the rest for her own benefit: "I'm afraid a door's going to get *you*."

She left the room, leaving Big Ed to ponder: "What'd I do wrong?" Ah, but you know, don't you, dear reader?

—

It was a struggle just to breathe. Its breath was raspy, its lungs awash in alcohol-based stain and three coats of varnish. It had endured a lot worse. Hurricanes, blizzards. **Hangings.** A little advanced carpentry wasn't going to stop it.

Ellen opened her eyes as soon as she heard it. She was a light sleeper and immediately woke at the sound.

Something was breathing inside her bedroom. Ellen reached for the small hurricane lamp on her bedside table and switched it on. The room remained in shadow. She lifted the blind, introducing additional light from a robust autumn moon. She had known where the sound was coming from (**just like you**). But now she could see it. The wardrobe door was swelling and retracting, swelling and retracting, the ragged rhythm of laboured breathing.

For a moment, Ellen considered that it just might be a Halloween prank. **'Tis the season and all that jazz.** But her father wasn't much of a prankster. And the details on the door were too exact. It was heaving to and fro, as if it was breathing, as if there were arteries pulsating throughout its frame. This wasn't a prop from Parties 4 Smarties. No, this was the real McCoy.

The door was alive.

And it sounded strangely familiar. Ellen realised that she'd heard it in the woods – as her friend lay dying. The door was making the sound of a dying witch.

Whatever apprehension Ellen might have had quickly vanished. She hopped off her bed, moving quickly across the furry pink carpet. The breathing grew stronger, healthier the closer she got. Ellen reached out to touch it. "It's okay." She stroked the wood with adoration. That seemed to soothe its laboured breathing.

She noticed a brass door handle shaped like a snake. "I'm coming in. Okay?"

But as she reached for the handle, the snake twisted and turned, opening the door on its own. Ellen didn't know what she expected to see. The inside of her wardrobe would have been a reasonable expectation. But the appearance of a breathing door seemed to rule out 'reasonable'. She was right, of course. The wardrobe wasn't there – no hanging jumpers or piles of shoes.

It was the entrance to another time.

Ellen was staring into the fabled woods of Salem, circa 1692. She could hear the crickets, the toads, a running brook, even over the sound of the door that breathed.

How? How was it possible? Was it a dream?

The voice in Ellen's head told her not to question what she saw, for it was the truth. It was time to trust her instincts.

CHAPTER EIGHT

She wasn't dreaming. In fact, for the first time in her life, Ellen was fully awake.

Ellen stepped through the doorway, following the electric-blue path into the woods. Even in the black of night, she could see. She saw the bugs and the beasts and all the creatures that thrived in the darkness. They were all around her. And they were beautiful!

Ellen felt free walking barefoot through the woods where she belonged. The trail would lead to the nemeton; that she knew. But what would she find there? That was a mystery, for Ellen had entered the woods of centuries past.

The great oak tree was the first thing she saw when she stepped into the clearing. It was back, in all its majesty, back where it belonged. And a second later she saw the figures. Three women. No, not *those* three. These women were seriously hideous, hunched over a cauldron and wearing hooded cloaks. Their skin had a deathly pallor, and their noses were long and beak-like. Two of them had sagging eyes. And they were the lookers! The third hag was eyeless. But hey, at least she had a mouth. The second one's mouth had been sewn shut with black thread.

The one in the middle, putrid in her own right but with

a working mouth and eyes, pointed a wand at the young intruder. She was their leader. "You, there! Come hither!"

The eyeless one drooled. She seemed hungry.

Now just a reminder: Ellen was brave, but she wasn't stupid. The stupid ones might 'come hither'. But not Ellen. She had no interest in *hithering*. Or making new friends with those strange women. So she turned and ran. Ellen ran for her life! The electric-blue trail disappeared and Ellen found herself running in circles, passing the same rocks, the same trees, again and again and again.

Until she found herself back in the nemeton, face to face with the hideous hags. Their leader reached out to touch her, stroking Ellen's fiery red hair with her spindly hand. Her fingers felt like spikes grazing Ellen's scalp. "Was it you, little one?"

"Who, me? What'd I do?"

The witch made a fist, pulling Ellen's hair. "Speak up! Who hath stolen our tree?" Ellen didn't answer, at least not yet. "Respond, little one! Or we shall collect thy tongue!"

The eyeless one gave a sniff. "Aaaah, fresh tongue. Such a delicacy."

The leader snatched Ellen's wrist, pulling her near the cauldron. Ellen could feel the searing heat, the bubbling

CHAPTER EIGHT

liquid inches from her blemish-free skin. She could see bones mixed in what resembled beef chilli way past its sell-by date.

Ellen pulled away. She had no intention of becoming the next ingredient. "I didn't steal anything!" she cried.

"Who then, child? Who hath removed the sacred tree from the nemeton?"

Ellen wanted to say she had no idea. Instead she blurted out the truth. "It was my father! He cut it down!"

"Oh, did he now?"

The third hag excitedly ripped the stitches from her mouth, wiping pus and bile on her sleeve. "A woodcutter's daughter! Bring forth the guilty one. We shall feast on his eyes!"

"Tomorrow night," declared the leader. "He must stand before us. During the feast of Samhain. He shall answer for his crimes!"

"But – but... he's my father."

The three witches got a great kick out of that one and roared with laughter. Oh, such pleasant memories, thinking back to the day they ate their own fathers. "Bring forth thy woodcutter. Or suffer the consequences!" The leader shoved Ellen's hand into the cauldron. She bit her lip, trying to fight through it. But the pain was too great and Ellen screamed.

And the witches – they cackled. They enjoyed a good scream.

Ellen woke up in bed, screaming. Big Ed was in her room in seconds. He flipped on the light. "You okay, Elle?"

It took her a moment to regroup. "Fine, Pop. Just a bad dream, that's all."

He sat on the bed. "You want to talk about it?" He glanced back at the door, which, for the moment, was not breathing. "It's my fault. I'm pig-headed, like your mother used to say. I'll take that door down – pronto!" He headed towards his toolbox.

"No, Pop, just leave it!"

"What's got into you? You're shivering." But Ellen couldn't tell him the truth, that behind the door that breathed were three witches looking to make a meal of him. The Big Ed Special.

"It's fine, Pop. Seriously. Let's talk about it tomorrow."

He approached the wardrobe and placed his hand on the serpent-shaped handle.

"No, Pop, no!"

Something stopped him. A smile. A memory. He released the handle and turned. "I'll bring you some warm milk. It's what she used to bring me when I couldn't sleep.

CHAPTER EIGHT

Your mother. I miss her, ya know. I miss her more than you can imagine."

"I know, Pop. I *can* imagine."

He walked towards the hallway. "I'm sorry about those things I said earlier. You know I love you, princess. You'll always be my princess."

"I know," said Ellen. *And you'll be the main ingredient of a witches' stew if you don't get out of here fast!* "Goodnight, Pop," she said, and turned out the light. As soon as he was gone, she checked her hand. *Ouch!* It stung. Ellen had been scalded for real.

The following day, Ellen skipped play rehearsals and headed into town. She needed some expert advice. Where does one find a witch expert? In *your* neighbourhood? Tall order. In Salem Village, finding a witch expert is like finding a World o' Coffee. They're on every corner.

Bella's Witch & Wizardry Shoppe wasn't the fanciest shop on the street – Merlin's Magic Shop, with its robotic rooftop display, had earned that title – but it was the one shop Ellen felt a connection to. So trusting her instincts, she went inside.

The shopkeeper was Bella herself, a middle-aged lady

wearing a pointed hat and a purple robe with a five-pointed star on the back. "Bright blessings," she said as Ellen stepped through the entrance. "How may I help you?"

Ellen looked around. There were jars filled with lizards' tails on one side of the store, high-quality witch and wizard memorabilia on the other. To stay competitive Bella targeted the naturalists as well as the tourists and wizarding book fans. Before Ellen could respond… "Let me guess. You've got a role in *The Crucible* and you want to learn all about witches?"

"Well, I am in *The Crucible*."

"Aha!" Bella tapped her own nose. "When you've got it, you've got it."

"But I'm not researching witches for the school play. I'm researching witches for real."

Bella saw the serious intent in Ellen's eyes. The young girl needed real help; it was obvious. Bella removed her pointed hat. "Follow me." She parted a beaded curtain, beckoning Ellen to follow. Ellen hesitated. "Come, come, I won't bite you." Maybe they all say that, especially the biters, but Ellen didn't have a lot of time. For her father's sake, she went with her instincts again, following Bella to a room in the back.

The room was loaded with out-of-print hardbacks, some old, others older. But no ghost stories. They were housed elsewhere. Heh. "You'll find all the answers you need in here." Ellen eyed the massive collection. There were far too many books to get through. It would take days, maybe even weeks, just to look at them all. And she didn't have weeks; she had hours. A door chime jingled and Bella excused herself to tend to the customer.

Ellen flipped through three or four books before tugging at her hair in frustration. The task was overwhelming. She needed to calm down. To find her centre. To visualise. Ellen removed her shoes and sat cross-legged on the floor. She closed her eyes, clearing her mind of worry. And soon she felt lighter than air.

Ellen felt like she was floating. And when she opened her eyes, she was. But that was *impossible*. She blinked hard – twice – and when she opened her eyes again, she was sitting cross-legged on the floor with an oversized book in her lap. It was called *The History of Salem Witches*. She feverishly began flipping through its yellowed pages, trusting that the information she needed would find her.

And it did.

There were entire chapters devoted to ancient rites and rituals. Some of the passages were downright disturbing. Flipping through the pages, Ellen perused a gruesome shopping list of forbidden spells and dark incantations. There were arcane etchings depicting scenes of human sacrifice and wanton destruction. There were portrayals of nightmare-inducing transformations, of innocent human beings writhing in pain as their malicious tormentors altered their forms into goats and toads. And there were vivid descriptions of the four great Sabbaths, witches' holidays that occurred throughout the year. There was one for each season, the most venerable one taking place on the 31st of October: Samhain, the witches' new year, as it was known by the Celts. A night when the dead were given free rein to walk the earth and when sacrifices, human and otherwise, were carried out in the name of evil. A night that had come to be known as… Halloween.

Ellen couldn't imagine the girls she had met in the woods acting like the witches from the book. She called out to the shop's owner, and Bella confirmed: "There are two types of witches in this world. Most, like me, are nature lovers. Powerful, yet peaceful."

Ellen had to ask. "And the other kind?"

"Beware. The second type is a force to be feared. These witches use their powers strictly in the service of darkness. Look." Bella turned to a page featuring a wood etching from

CHAPTER EIGHT

1692. It showed three hags – the *same* witches Ellen had seen on her midnight stroll. They were preparing a human sacrifice. The main course was floating in a cauldron, wearing a face she recognised. It was Ellen's father, Big Ed.

Ellen clapped her hand over her mouth, muffling a scream. Bella, on the other hand, let one rip. A scream, that is. What she saw in the etching was beyond her comprehension.

"What do you see?" asked Ellen.

"It's what I *don't* see," said Bella. "The picture. It's changed."

"How do you mean?"

Bella pointed to the clearing. "There used to be a tree here. A magnificent oak had always been a part of this picture."

Ellen shuddered. "And now it's gone."

That night in her room, Ellen was watching the clock as closely as she watched the wardrobe door. Midnight was fast approaching. The witching hour. Samhain. Halloween! Soon the horrible hags would be demanding their sacrifice, her father the preferred choice. But *The History of Salem Witches* had offered her an alternative. It wasn't a great alternative, mind you, but it was all she had. Ellen had come across an obscure witches' rite that would enable her to undo the sacrifice. Sort of. For the sake of her father, the pig-headed lout she loved so dearly, Ellen had to try.

The clock struck twelve. It was Halloween. Ellen gulped. Nothing happened. The door remained a door. One minute passed. Then two. Ellen wondered if it had all been a dream. But at three minutes past midnight, two things put a stop to her happy thought. One, her arm began to throb. And two...

The door began to breathe.

Ellen got up from her bed and approached it. The door was heaving, splitting, growing stronger. And the handle was no longer a handle. It was *alive* – a living serpent coiled in a knot. Ellen froze, not wanting to grasp it. Then the door flew open on its own, inviting her to return to the wicked woods of 1692.

Once more she stepped through a portal that had once been her wardrobe, and entered a world where time had no meaning. The woods of Salem were themselves timeless, as timeless as the wind and the water and the fire and the trees. By then Ellen didn't need an electric-blue path. She knew where she was going. She knew the trail by heart. This was her third trek, after all. And the third time's the... oh, never mind.

Ellen bravely entered the nemeton to discover a great celebration already under way. The clearing was filled with masked celebrants dancing round a bonfire. Witches, all of them. And this was their holiday. Samhain. Halloween. A time when the veil between the living and the dead is tissue thin.

Ellen shoved her way through the crowd. Several witches turned and pointed. "Is it she? The witch who destroyed our tree?"

"I am not a witch!" Ellen replied contemptuously.

She arrived at the cauldron, presenting herself to the three hags.

"Where is thy woodcutter?" asked the leader.

Ellen looked the evil crone in the eye. "The woodcutter isn't coming! You'll have to settle for me."

"Have you no fear, child?"

"Of course I have fear. I'm scared to death. But that isn't enough to sacrifice my own father." Ellen took a breath before invoking the ancient rite. "I offer myself willingly, in accordance with the laws of your society. Take *me* as your sacrifice."

"You're a fool," scoffed the leader. "Take her!"

The celebrants roared with excitement, dancing and cavorting. If the revised menu seemed, at first, a disappointment to the demonic diners – after all, Ellen didn't have nearly as much meat on her bones as her father – there were other compensations. The young ones were usually stronger, which meant more time in the pot tenderising. The meat would literally drip off the bone. Oh, and the screams. The young ones also came with healthier lungs.

"So mote it be," said the leader.

"Into the cauldron, my dear," added the eyeless one.

But Ellen refused to climb in on her own. True, true, she had made the offer. She had agreed to be cooked and eaten alive. But sorry, witches. She wasn't going to dive in without a fight. If they wanted her, they'd have to come get her.

So mote it be.

Ellen ran, but there were too many of them. A sea of hands reached out and grabbed her, snatching her round the waist. The celebrants lifted her above their heads, carrying her to the cauldron like she was crowd-surfing at a concert.

"In she goes," said the eyeless one.

The celebrants shoved Ellen into the cauldron, bare feet first. The stew was not yet hot. And that was when she realised that they intended to cook her slowly. One of the witches stoked the flames and they danced higher, hotter – first yellow, then blue. The pot would come to a boil, along with

CHAPTER EIGHT

Ellen, the main ingredient. She closed her eyes and thought of her father. And from there, she thought of her mother. What would *she* have done? And a voice entered Ellen's head.

It was telling her to float.

Ellen closed her eyes and visualised. She saw herself rising, lighter than air. And suddenly, it was reality. She felt her body rising, leaving the pot, ascending above the cauldron, her feet dripping with stew. Down below, the celebrants pointed. "Look! She floats! The woodcutter's daughter! She floats!"

"Come down from there!" growled the lead witch. "Into the pot, little one!" The celebrants leapt to grab her, clawing at her ankles. *Just a little higher*, Ellen thought. And it happened. Higher she went, just as she pictured it.

But the leader remained unimpressed. "Get down from there at once! We demand our sacrifice. A life for our tree!" Of all the witches, it was the eyeless one who reached up with her spindly hand and latched on to Ellen's ankle, yanking her down, down, like a balloon running out of air. The celebrants overpowered Ellen, swarming her. They bound her legs and began preparing their sacrifice once more. Her situation appeared hopeless. Ellen closed her eyes, resigned to her fate, until —

Brrrrrrummm! Brrrrrrummm!

What was that? The celebrants grew quiet, and the witches turned in the direction of the unknown sound. *Brrrrrrummm! Brrrrrrummm!* It sounded like a monstrous battle cry, not of their time. It had invaded their sacred celebration. But it wasn't a ghost, a goblin or a ghoul.

It was the woodcutter, Ellen's father. He stood at the entrance of the nemeton. And he had brought along his plus one… Mr Do-Right.

Brrrrrrummm! Brrrrrrummm!

"Run, Pop!" Ellen shouted from the cauldron.

"Not without you, Elle." Big Ed stormed the clearing, wielding his chainsaw like a wild man. The celebrants backed away, frightened by the mechanical monster, allowing him to make it unscathed all the way to the cauldron – to his daughter – where the three horrible witches were standing guard.

"I'm the one you want. I cut down your tree. And I'm sorry. Truly sorry. But let my daughter go now, or there will be trouble."

The eyeless witch turned towards the woodcutter. "We demand a sacrifice. The girl shall live, but only if *you* take her place."

CHAPTER EIGHT

Ellen's father glanced back at the coven. He was larger than the largest witch – they didn't call him Big Ed for nothing, you know – but he was also outnumbered. He looked at his daughter and knew that, as her father, he still had a responsibility to protect her and teach her. And it was his responsibility to accept the consequences of his actions, even if his actions had consequences that dated back to 1692.

The eyeless one licked her lips. Big Ed was the meatier choice, by far. And judging from his sweaty scent, he had already been seasoned. She wasted no more time. "Into the pot, woodcutter!" It was an order.

"First set my daughter free."

The leader nodded. "So mote it be." The witches lifted Ellen from the pot and cut her bindings. She immediately ran to her father and hugged him. Big Ed gently pushed her away with one arm and handed her the chainsaw with the other.

"Pop, what are you doing?"

"The only thing a father can do. Be a hero to his little girl."

"You've never stopped being my hero!"

Big Ed put an arm round his daughter one last time and kissed the top of her head. Then he whispered in her ear, "I love you, princess. Now, keep this pointed at them and use it to get back home. Go!"

The witches moved forwards, demanding what they were owed. And Big Ed never went back on a deal. He lifted his leg, taking the first step into the cauldron. The mixture was now hot. He could feel the heat closing in on him, a horrifying way to end his life, but it would be worth it for his daughter. Saving Ellen was the bargain of the century. Four centuries, in fact.

Ellen pleaded with the witches. "Let him go! He said he was sorry. Now let him go!"

" 'He said he was sorry,' " mocked the eyeless one. "For that, we should go hungry?"

"I think not," said the leader.

But Ellen couldn't leave. It was up to her to save her father's life. She turned to face the witches, inhaled, exhaled and then, in her best stage voice, issued a direct threat: "I'm warning you."

The witches cackled, and their leader responded. "Warning us? You have no dominion here. Float away, little one. Before we add you to our feast."

CHAPTER EIGHT

The sweat was pouring from Big Ed's face. "Go, Ellen! Run! *Run!*"

But Ellen disobeyed, no longer blindly following orders. "I'm going to say it one last time," she stated calmly. "Release the woodcutter or pay the penalty." Again, the witches cackled in response. Ellen raised her magic mechanical monster from the twenty-first century, Mr Do-Right, and charged.

Brrrrrummm! Brrrrrummm!

The very next morning, Big Ed removed the door from Ellen's wardrobe, and together they returned it to the clearing where the tree once stood. Two girls – one blonde and one brunette – watched from the opposite side of the clearing. When the task was completed, they nodded knowingly to Ellen. They were three once more.

Later, Ellen returned *The History of Salem Witches* to Bella's Witch & Wizardry Shoppe. Bella held Ellen's gaze for an extended time. She knew. She knew what Ellen *really* was. She was a witch – one of the good kinds, just like Abigail. "Thank you," Ellen said as she returned the book. "This changed my life."

"I know," Bella replied. "Come back soon, my pretty," she added with a wink. Ellen smiled and left, knowing that she would return. On her own, Bella opened the book, turning to the wood etching from 1692. It had changed once more. It now depicted a young warrior princess – defending her father from a coven of evil witches. In her hands was a strange mechanical device.

So mote it be.

Chapter Nine

TWO OUT OF THREE AIN'T BAD

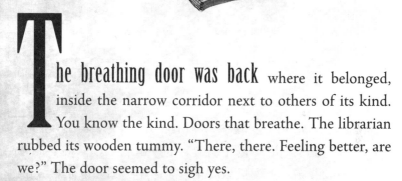

The breathing door was back where it belonged, inside the narrow corridor next to others of its kind. You know the kind. Doors that breathe. The librarian rubbed its wooden tummy. "There, there. Feeling better, are we?" The door seemed to sigh yes.

Marge and Pasquale had seen and heard enough. They were already looking for another way out. They bolted through the corridor and ran down a grand staircase. But the librarian was waiting at the bottom. They ran back up to the top. The librarian was there, too. In each direction they ran, Amicus Arcane was somehow standing in their path.

"We want to leave!" shouted Marge at the top of her lungs. "We didn't do anything wrong! You can't keep us here! Please!"

"But you can't leave," replied the librarian. "Not without this." He slid his gloved hand into his jacket. Marge and Pasquale backed away, holding hands, anticipating the horror. What was he reaching for? What would it be? A beating heart, perhaps? Tobe's ears? The brain of Declan Smythe? It was certainly small enough to fit.

But no, not quite.

The librarian removed a musty old wallet from his inside pocket. He opened it and began counting out money. "Your final payment."

Pasquale's van made its way through the grounds of the mansion, minus three crates and one burly passenger. Marge and Pasquale at first said nothing. The shock hadn't worn off. They couldn't be sure about any of what they'd seen or heard. Except the part about Declan Smythe. He was missing for real.

"The fog's lifting." It was Pasquale breaking the silence. "It'll be dawn soon." Marge looked his way and smiled. She was attractive – even beautiful – once you got to know her. "He'll be okay, right?"

CHAPTER NINE

Marge hadn't stopped smiling. "Declan? He always has been. I expect he'll turn up at the Raven's Inn looking for his share."

"You wanna have breakfast with me, Marjorie? My treat."

She nodded. "Sure. I'll have breakfast with you."

It had been a strange night, filled with supernatural sonatas, ancient curses and a witches' Sabbath. What was real and what was imagined they did not know. But breakfast was going to taste good.

The van continued down the twisting, winding, curving path, slowing by the cemetery. The gravediggers were just finishing their shift. A single oversized casket was being lowered into a fresh grave. "Hey, Pask, what do you suppose happened to the other two?"

Indeed, the other two graves remained untouched.

"Who knows? Maybe it ain't our business to know."

"Or anyone else's," added Marge. With that, she reached into her bag, pulled out the map made from you-know-what and tossed it out the window. A sudden breeze lifted the map high into the air and over the mansion's front gate to Amicus Arcane, who was waiting at the entrance.

As if in response, Pasquale hit the accelerator. He wanted nothing more than to distance himself from that gated mansion on the hill. The last thing they saw on that unforgettable night was a scene they'd one day describe to their grandchildren: three motley hitch-hikers still looking to bum a ride, except these hitch-hikers were most definitely not in the pink, if you get our meaning.

Pasquale turned to Marge. "Should we?"

She shook her head. "No way. Keep going!"

Pasquale quickly sped up, racing past them. As he did, he caught sight in his mirror of the librarian, who now stood by the mansion gate. He was calling after the hitch-hikers. Calling them back home. Just then, a burly figure joined them. He had bulging biceps and one good eye.

And he was glowing.

Hereafter Thoughts

Ah, there you are!

Safe and as snug as a bug in a slug.
Unlike Declan Smythe, who learnt
this valuable lesson the hard way:

Never take something that isn't yours,
lest something that isn't yours take you.
Heh-heh-heh.

What's that I hear? Our clock is striking thirteen.
It is time for the grim grinning ghosts to come out to socialise.
It is also time for me to split. Or is it splat?
Until we meet again, foolish reader...
dream big, SCREAM BIGGER!

Oh, and there's a little matter I forgot to mention:

Beware of hitch-hiking ghosts.

———— ✿ ————

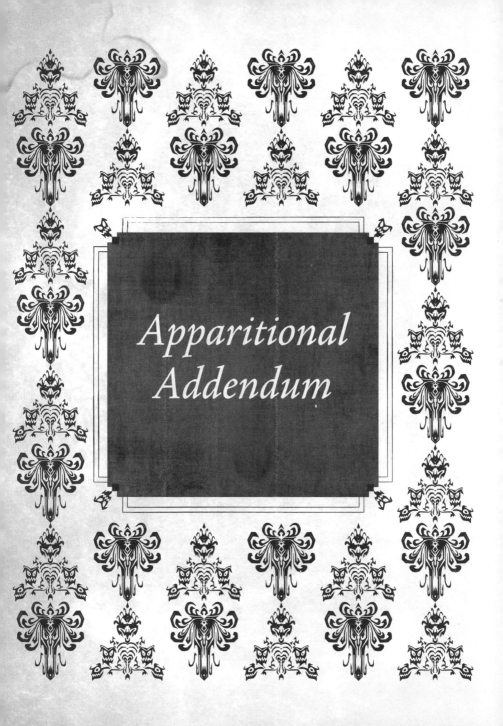

Apparitional Addendum

You didn't heed my warnings,
and now it's too late.

Look behind you, if you dare.
Go on, take a peek.

There seems to be nothing there.
Oh, but there is, I assure you.

You needn't bother to look again.
As I've told you, it's too late.

Something has already followed you home!

———— ❧ ————

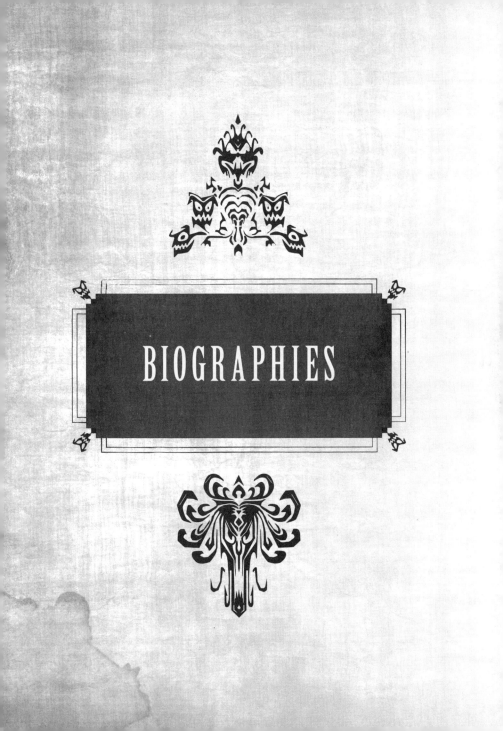

BIOGRAPHIES

Amicus Arcane *Little is known about the dearly departed Amicus Arcane, save for his love of books. As the mansion librarian, both in this life and in the afterlife, Amicus has delighted in all forms of the written word. However, this librarian's favourite tales are those of terror and suspense. After all, there is nothing better to ease a restless spirit than a frightfully good ghost story.*

John Esposito *When John Esposito met Amicus Arcane on a midnight stroll through New Orleans Square, he was so haunted by the librarian's tales that he decided to transcribe them for posterity. John has worked in both film and television, on projects such as* Stephen King's Graveyard Shift, R. L. Stine's The Haunting Hour, Teen Titans, *and the* Walking Dead *web series, for which he won consecutive Writer's Guild Awards. John lives in New York with his wife and children and still visits with Amicus from time to time.*

Kelley Jones *For the illustrations accompanying his terrifying tales, Amicus Arcane approached Kelley Jones, an artist with a scary amount of talent. Kelley has worked for every major comic book publisher but is best known for his definitive work on Batman for DC Comics. Kelley lives in Northern California with his wife and children and hears from Amicus every October 31, whether he wants to or not.*

DEAD END!
Prepare to exit
to the Living World